THE
MISEDUCATION
OF
HENRY
CANE

A NOVEL

CHARLES BROOKS

MILLENNIAL PRINT

SIMON & SCHUSTER

NEW YORK LONDON TORONTO SYDNEY NEW DELHI

Simon & Schuster
1230 Avenue of the Americas
New York, NY 10020

First Simon & Schuster hardcover edition August 2019

For information about special discounts for bulk purchases, please contact Simon & Schuster Special Sales at 1-866-506-1949 or business@simonandschuster.com.

The Simon & Schuster Speakers Bureau can bring authors to your live event. For more information or to book an event, contact the Simon & Schuster Speakers Bureau at 1-866-248-3049 or visit our website at www.simonspeakers.com.

Interior design by Carly Loman

Manufactured in the United States of America

10 9 8 7 6 5 4 3 2 1

Library of Congress Cataloging-in-Publication Data

Names: Brooks, Charles (Fictitious character) author.
Title: The miseducation of Henry Cane / Charles Brooks.
Description: New York : Simon & Schuster, 2019. | Includes bibliographical references and index.
Identifiers: LCCN 2019013517 (print) | LCCN 2019017708 (ebook) | ISBN 9781982129644 (Ebook) | ISBN 9781982129637 (hardback) | ISBN 9781982129620 (trade paperback)
Subjects: LCSH: Young men—Fiction. | Middle-aged women—Fiction. | May-December romances—Fiction. | Younger (Television program) | BISAC: FICTION / Contemporary Women. | FICTION / Humorous. | FICTION / Media Tie-In. | GSAFD: Love stories | Bildungsromans
Classification: LCC PS3616.I214 (ebook) | LCC PS3616.I214 M57 2019 (print) | DDC 813/.6—dc23
LC record available at https://lccn.loc.gov/2019013517

ISBN 978-1-9821-2963-7
ISBN 978-1-9821-2964-4 (ebook)

To Liza,
who taught me the value of
telling the truth

THE
MISEDUCATION
OF
HENRY
CANE

PROLOGUE

I wasn't raised to be a liar. I was raised to be a good son, a good friend, a Princeton man, a publisher, someone's boss, someone's devoted husband, a child's caring father.

And yet, this summer, my lies nearly derailed all of it.

My memory of the night before was hazy and disjointed, but I knew I was to blame for every terrible thing that happened. I sat up and rubbed at my eyes. Judging from the position of the sun I'd been asleep on the beach for quite some time.

My recollections came in waves. Fishing, drinking, crashing the party, the disgusting words that came out of my mouth, getting smacked across the face. The way she looked at me. The way he looked at me. Shame knotted my insides. How had I let it go so far? I wasn't this person.

But I'd become a different person with her.

CHAPTER ONE

Two months earlier . . . June 1, 1994

"Will you miss me?"

Caroline had asked me this twice already, and each time I gave her the required "Yes, of course . . . very much."

I wondered if she'd ask a fourth time, and I told myself that if she did I'd come up with something more clever. In fact, I started practicing witty things I could say in my mind, but they all sounded cheesy and lame, so we rode the rest of the way in silence.

Before she got out of the car at the British Airways doors at JFK I gave her an awkward hug, because, for all intents and purposes, we'd broken up the night before in a very courteous and official way. She'd be spending the summer in London interning with the Royal Shakespeare Company and hoped to stay on in the fall as an associate producer. We'd gone back and forth for months about the idea of staying together. I needed her to be the one to break it off. I'd always been terrible at making big decisions. If I'm being honest I was used to women making all my decisions for me: first my mom, then Caroline. I'm not gonna lie about the fact that I liked it. I functioned best when things just sort of happened to me. When Caroline finally announced we were definitely calling it quits, in an act that involved plenty of tears and bold proclamations about what we both really deserved and needed, she told me she still wanted me to be the one to see her off at the airport. I'd never once told her no during the course of our three-year relationship, and I saw no reason to start.

I carried her luggage to the curbside check-in and tipped the guy there twenty bucks for no real reason except I wanted Caroline's last image of me to be me handing off her bags and tipping some guy too much. She leaned in and kissed me goodbye on the side of my mouth the way you'd accidentally kiss an elderly aunt.

Caroline Alby. I'd loved her the moment I set eyes on her, but by the time I was back on the Long Island Expressway I felt a strange relief, the kind of feeling that comes when winter becomes spring and you get to take off a too-heavy and too-itchy sweater. I would have stayed with Caroline as long as she wanted me to. I hadn't known the freedom would feel both sweet and terrifying.

My mother kept threatening to sell our beach house. Every single June that I can remember, Deidre Cane packed two suitcases for each of us and drove the three hours from our town house on East Eighty-Third Street to the beach house in Sag Harbor. Once she was there she flung open all the windows, wiped her finger through the collected winter dust, and declared, "We should get rid of this old wreck and get an apartment in Paris."

For a long time I believed that was actually what she wanted. Only in my teen years did I understand it was sarcasm or maybe irony. It took a while before I became fairly certain my mother just enjoyed being unhappy.

The house, a weather-beaten colonial revival, had certainly seen better days, but it wasn't a wreck by any means. This was the Hamptons after all. The peeling paint and the floors that forever smelled a little like salt, sand, and damp towels only made me love it more. I knew my mother secretly took pride in our rickety old house with its musty furniture. Old-money houses out east tended to have an up-market thrift-store decorative style, whereas new-money houses were all white leather and sharp edges. I once attended a party with my parents at the home of this Internet millionaire. That's what everyone was calling him, "that Internet millionaire," like it was a strange sort of profession, an encyclopedia salesman or that guy who sells you potions out of a briefcase. "That Internet millionaire" helped build Prodigy or had a diaper delivery service you ordered through AOL or something like that.

"It looks like it was decorated by a Colombian drug lord," one of my mother's friends said to another woman. "And not even one of the interesting ones."

But this summer, Deidre had gotten her Parisian wish, or at least a taste of it. My father had been invited to teach a summer session at the Sorbonne, something about publishing the great American novel, and Mother said if he didn't take it she was finally going to leave him for Stan the butcher, a man she insisted knew how to take a damn vacation. How she knew anything intimate about Stan, a man who also had a lazy eye and was missing a canine tooth, was beyond me, but Mother did have the ability to talk to anyone about anything, and maybe she'd managed to unlock secrets about Stan beyond how he trimmed a pork shank.

My father suggested renting out our old house at the beach, but my mother wouldn't hear of it.

"Strangers putting their filthy feet on my furniture," she scoffed.

"I thought you couldn't stand *that wreck of a place* anyway," my father replied with a bemused smile.

"It's my wreck, and I don't want anyone else in it. Henry will spend the summer there before he starts work with you in the fall. Let him relax a little before you and the cutthroat world of publishing break his spirit."

I couldn't object. Having the beach house all to myself for the entire summer was a better plan than staying in our place in the city, which, by the way, was also the complete opposite of a wreck—a four-floor town house with actual servants' quarters. There hadn't been any servants in the house since at least the turn of the last century, but the quarters were still there all the same. Mother used them for storing holiday ornaments and one time for an au pair from Germany who Deidre said smelled like sauerkraut.

Their house wouldn't be my house for that much longer. Beginning in September I had a lease on a studio on West Eighth Street. I would never say out loud that I wanted to escape the Upper East Side. I just wanted something new, something different. And maybe a part of me liked the fact that my mother didn't love trekking below Fourteenth Street unless she was picking up whitefish from Russ & Daughters.

Relaxation was a foreign concept to my father, but because my mother was keen on it he accepted it and Paris all the same. I'm fairly certain I inherited my desperate need to please beautiful women from him.

It took only two hours to get to the beach from the airport. That's what happens when you leave on a Wednesday afternoon. I rolled all the windows down and indulged in the guilty pleasure of singing at the top of my lungs to the entire CD of Madonna's greatest hits, which Caroline had left in the six-disc changer. I hadn't exactly forgotten to remind her about it.

Nothing had changed about the beach house since I'd seen it last September, and its sameness comforted me. By the time I opened all the windows and swiped away enough of the dust from the furniture, I had no idea what I wanted to do next. Endless days of nothing stretched ahead of me. I had a stack of novels I'd been meaning to read, and part of me relished the idea of staying put in the house for an entire week as I made my way through them in delicious silence.

I didn't get that luxury

"Hey, dildo."

Sperry never knocked. He hadn't knocked since he started wandering into our beach house when he was five years old. It's how we became friends—he just wandered on into a stranger's house. His parents bought the place next door, and they were the kind of parents who had no trouble setting their child loose on the neighborhood while they unpacked. He came right into our kitchen, opened our fridge, and made himself a ham sandwich. My mother found him sitting at our kitchen table and sent him up to my room to play. That was how Deidre parented in the late seventies. Sperry was a real big kid. My mother called him husky and was always trying to get him to eat things like celery sticks with peanut butter and raisins, and instead he'd demand a sloppy joe.

It turned out he lived not too far from us in the city, and we both wound up at Collegiate for kindergarten through the twelfth grade. When I left for college in New Jersey, Sperry went to Dartmouth and made a big deal about how it was just his safety school, even though everyone knew his dad paid for a new wing at the main library to get him in. If I thought hard about it (and I tried not to), Sperry and I shouldn't still be friends. He'd grown into the kind of frat boy who would go down in Dartmouth history for rushing the field naked during the Ivy championships and doing a five-minute keg stand, whereas I could never even find the keg at most college parties. But it was easier to keep him around than to get rid of him. He was familiar and comfortable, like waffles or a crocheted quilt.

Sperry opened my freezer and turned back to look at me with disappointment in his puppy-like eyes.

"No ice cream."

"Haven't shopped yet."

How had it just occurred to me that I would need to go to the market and fill the refrigerator myself? The realization was both enlightening and embarrassing.

"I gotta eat, man."

"You know there's probably food at your house."

"There definitely isn't. Kelli-Anne is on a new diet where she doesn't eat things that have mass."

Kelli-Anne was Sperry's latest stepmom. She wasn't all that much older than us. In fact, we could have overlapped in high school. Sperry was saved that indignity. Kelli-Anne came from some small town in Texas.

Sperry mimicked Kelli-Anne's high-pitched, nasally twang. "Brett, you could stand to quit eatin' so much too. You're as fat as a sow ready for slaughter." He placed one hand on either side of his formidable gut and shook it like he was a mall Santa Claus. Nobody but Sperry's parents called him by his given name, Brett. We called him Sperry since he owned more boat shoes than anyone I'd ever met. No one had ever seen anything else on his feet. Not even when he was just a chubby kid raiding my mother's fridge.

"Come on. Let's get out of this house. Let's get crabs," Sperry insisted.

"You had them. Remember junior year." That was a joke that didn't get old.

"You're funny. At least I got laid in high school. Nothing a little antibiotic didn't clear up. Let's go." He was already halfway out the door. "We'll take the boat and get some good claws across the bay."

By *the* boat he meant *my* boat, which should have irritated me, but I let it go.

"You want to go all the way over to Greenport?" I complained.

"They taste better out there. So do the beers. And the girls are prettier."

"The girls out there just don't know you. That makes them prettier," I countered. "You haven't done anything to offend them yet."

"Touché. Come on, dildo. I'm starving."

My boat wasn't anything special. But it was all mine, every single piece of her. I started building her from scratch when I was thirteen years old. My grandfather was alive back then, and the only thing he wanted to do besides work was show me how to build a wooden boat, a childhood dream of his. Her name was *Arabella*, from the Captain Blood pirate stories, which I read when I was way too young to be reading them because they were filled with blood and guts and nasty men doing nasty things. My *Arabella* was a flat-bottomed skiff made entirely out of sweet chestnut, and, in my opinion, she was only getting better with age. I didn't let just anyone go out on the boat. I'd never once taken a girl out on her; it would feel curiously unfaithful.

The water was smooth as glass, and the tides were in our favor to whip us around Shelter Island and over to the North Fork in less than an hour.

Sperry removed his salmon-pink polo shirt and let his pasty chest bake in the midafternoon sun, stretching his arms skyward. That was another difference between the two of us. I preferred to keep my shirt on unless I was planning on swimming, showering, or getting with a girl. At the age of twenty-one I was the rare man who still slept in a pair of pajamas bought by my mother. Sperry liked to be naked as often as possible.

"This summer is gonna rule," he shouted, even though I was well within earshot. Like me, Sperry was taking a break for the summer before he'd start a job his dad got for him in the mergers and acquisitions department of Goldman. Unlike me, Sperry was wildly excited about his life come September. Sperry had never wanted to do anything but work in M&A at Goldman. It's what his dad had been doing for the past thirty years and what his grandfather did for fifty years before that.

I knew I should feel grateful that I had such a good job lined up for me. I'm not one of those people who take these kinds of things for granted. Still, I was less enthusiastic about my future working for my father than Sperry was. I also wasn't even that excited for the next two months. I knew this summer would be exactly like every summer we had at the beach. That's the thing about the Hamptons. It's all about the same people doing the same things in the same places and then pretending something new and interesting was happening.

Sperry kept going on and on about his plans for our epic season. His specialty was making plans. In another life, another world, he should have been an event or wedding planner, maybe a hotel concierge, not a corporate banker.

"Johnson's cousin is bouncing at the Sand Trap and he promised to let us cut the line as long as we bring some hot chicks. I feel like Beth is pretty hot, and she's got enough decent-looking friends to get us in all summer." Beth was Sperry's stepsister from his dad's third marriage, the shortest marriage of the five, and the two of them never actually lived under the same roof, which is probably why it was so easy for Sperry to constantly fantasize about taking off her clothes.

"It's still creepy when you talk about how hot Beth is," I said.

Sperry flipped his palms toward the blazing sun.

"I can't help it. The heart wants what the heart wants." He pounded on his chest like he was Tarzan and did a cannonball off the boat and into the water, making a splash that forced me to hold tight to the steering wheel.

Because it was a Wednesday we found a spot to dock right next to this place called the Feisty Crab and Sperry was out of the boat before I could even tie her up. By the time I got to the table he'd ordered a basket of fries, clam strips, crab legs, and two frosty mugs of beer. The Feisty Crab was small and warm, with taxidermy fish and photos of fishermen covering the wooden walls. The crowd, even on a weekday, was feistier than the crab, which, to be honest, was perfectly serviceable, but not any better than a crab we could have ordered in Sag Harbor or Montauk. It was absolutely better than anything we could get in East Hampton, where all the food was the same as country-club food the world over: overcooked chicken, frozen crab legs, and enormous rubbery shrimp covered in ketchup that someone claimed was cocktail sauce.

The Feisty Crab's menu consisted of things that came directly out of the ocean and other things that had been dropped in a deep fryer for approximately seven minutes.

"I'm in love with the waitress," Sperry informed me as we dug into our food.

"Which one?"

"That sloe-eyed goddess who just wiped the crab crumbs off the table." He pointed with his chubby index finger.

"She's pretty," I said, because Sperry likes validation and because it was true.

"Man. Are you still hung up on Caroline? She's definitely boning a Frenchman at thirty thousand feet as we speak."

I didn't tell him I'd imagined the same thing as I pulled away from JFK. I took a long sip of my beer instead.

"Nah. I'm just getting reacclimated to being a single man." That was true. Caroline was only the second woman I'd ever slept with, a fact Sperry may have thought but not known for sure. Contrary to his previous jest, I did have sex in high school, I just didn't talk about it the way Sperry did all the time. I'd done it seven times to be exact, with the same girl—Annie Westover. And then I met Caroline the first day of freshman orientation. We weren't exactly strangers. We had circled each other for years in various Manhattan and Hamptons social circles, but that icebreaker session in Annenberg Hall was the first time we'd ever spoken to each other beyond *Hey* and *Are you spending the summer out east?* It turned out we were in the same microeconomics section, a requirement that neither of us had any interest in. We sat next to each other there because we'd already developed a vague familiarity. I became her study buddy for all of freshman year. I figured spending time in her dorm room was better than staying in my own double and

listening to my roommate have loud sex with Michiko, our Japanese RA. Caroline dated this guy named Carter for the entire first
semester. Carter happened to be the Princeton quarterback and
the lead baritone in the campus's most adored a cappella group. It
probably doesn't mean much anywhere else, but at an Ivy League
college the Venn intersection of football player with a cappella geek
is equivalent to a Mount Olympus–level god. But Carter broke her
heart when he fell for the second-string baritone. I pretended to
be incredibly surprised, let her cry on my shoulder, and delivered
pints of rocky road to her dorm room every night for a week. My
persistent presence eventually wore her down, and sometime during sophomore year she started calling me her boyfriend, and that
was that. I think she knew I would never break her heart.

Sperry pulled a paper wrapper halfway off a straw and then
blew it into my face. "Earth to dildo! You can ask the waitress
out if you want to. I'm a very good friend. I'm chivalrous. Like a
knight." He raised his arm as if he were pulling out an imaginary
sword and managed to knock all the condiments off the table.
Sperry's first beer was already gone, and he was twirling his index
finger in the air to summon another.

I picked up the wrapper and threw it back in his general direction, letting it settle in the dregs of his beer glass. "All yours. I'm
not big on long-distance. But this is a logistically tricky romance
for you. How will you get across the bay without a boat? You gonna
drive all the way around Riverhead?"

"You'll bring me, man. This is all we have to do for the entire
summer."

The thought of doing this every day with Sperry felt worse than
the existential sameness of the rest of my life come September.

I took this class called Philosophy of the Twentieth-Century Man my junior year at Princeton. Being in the privileged position of knowing exactly what you're going to do with the rest of your life means you can take classes as frivolous and enjoyable as Philosophy of the Twentieth-Century Man. God, I loved that class. We spent nearly half the semester on Viktor Frankl and man's search for meaning. Of course we did. Frankl was pretty much the crux of man thinking about philosophy in the last hundred years. Caroline took the class too, and she hated it. Really hated it. "Why is it Twentieth-Century Man and not Woman?" she scoffed. I didn't have a good answer. She stopped going about three weeks in, a couple of days after it was too late to officially quit the class without getting an incomplete, which meant I took even more diligent notes to please her. I couldn't get enough of man's search for meaning. It was one of the few classes that really got stuck in my brain.

"Everything can be taken from a man but one thing: the last of the human freedoms—to choose one's attitude in any given set of circumstances, to choose one's own way."

Sitting at the Feisty Crab with Sperry I let Frankl's line pass through my mind a few times.

I wasn't paying attention to Sperry's slurry come-on to the waitress. "I seem to have lost my phone number. Can I have yours?" Her snorty laugh brought me back to reality.

That one usually worked with about 50 percent accuracy. I'd once said it aloud myself, just to hear how it sounded coming out of my mouth. I never said it again. Guys like me shouldn't say things like that.

"You seem like a guy who loses a lot of things." She reached into her pocket, pulled out a blank piece of paper, and wrote her name, Kelli, with a little heart over the *i*, and her number on it.

She got real chatty then. She was eighteen and would be start-ing classes at Hofstra in the fall. She grew up just a few streets over from here and wanted to study fashion design.

"You know Isaac Mizrahi is a family friend," Sperry bragged. "I could probably introduce you."

The famous fashion designer was actually a friend of Sperry's father's and not Sperry's. The only time I'd ever seen them inter-act was last summer at the Watermill Center benefit when Sperry passed out in the back seat of Mr. Mizrahi's car, thinking it was his own car. Mr. Mizrahi was not pleased, and I knew that he would not consider Sperry a friend at all.

Sperry then made a big show to Kelli of pointing across the water to indicate where we lived, on the *right* side of the bay. His pudgy digit became a laser pointer on a chart indicating relative wealth and success.

"When do you get off? Get on our boat." Now it was *our* boat. "And we'll all go out in Sag."

I shot him a severe glance. It was one thing to drive the boat back tipsy with just Sperry and me on it. Somehow that didn't worry me. I'd been keeping the two of us safe since Sperry learned how to huff on whipped cream cans in the eighth grade. But I hated having strangers on the boat. He knew it too. He avoided my eyes, knowing exactly what I was thinking.

"I'm hitting the bathroom," I said, and pushed my chair back a little too forcefully. It made a noise like fingernails scraping against a chalkboard, and that shut Sperry up for a second.

"You want another beer?"

"Sure. Whatever. But then we've got to get back."

Sperry rolled his eyes. "Because you've got so much to do, man." The Feisty Crab had only a single bathroom, and there was a line of mostly women waiting to use it. I supposed the men probably went outside and peed behind their cars in the parking lot or off the docks. I didn't actually consider doing it myself. I wish I could. But I was always terrified I would be caught by a well-appointed woman like my mother with my zipper down. That woman, dressed like Deidre, in her silk camisole, pink clam-diggers, and pearls would see me and my very average penis and scream or call for the police. Nope, I couldn't pee outside. Instead, I occupied myself by reading notes and ads pinned to the large community bulletin board next to the bathroom. An orange cat named Oscar had been missing for almost a month. A woman named Shana would clean your house for $9 an hour. The auxiliary club was hosting a bake sale for some guy named Rooster who needed help raising money for his chemotherapy treatments. An evening of poetry at the Last Drop Coffee Shop would be held on Thursday night.

An older woman, maybe in her forties, with chemically bleached blond hair came out of the bathroom. She wore a crop top revealing a tight tummy and a tattoo of a dolphin leaping over her navel.

"Toilet won't flush," she announced in a singsong voice to imply that the broken toilet was absolutely not her fault and everyone in line groaned. The next person waiting plugged her nose and went in anyway.

"Why don't you just pee off the pier?" a girl who couldn't be more than fifteen asked me.

"You know that's illegal."

"Pussy," she murmured under her breath.

I was about to abandon the line and just try to get Sperry back on the boat when a yellow-lined piece of paper caught my eye. It was pinned all the way in the top-left corner of the bulletin board, handwritten, and the ink was fading. A tearaway phone number was written five times vertically on the bottom.

FISHERMAN WANTED—No experience neccesary.

I first noticed that *necessary* was misspelled, and I had an intense desire to find a pen and correct the mistake. Then Frankl manifested again—though I actually heard it in Caroline's deep and husky voice this time, the one she'd used in my dorm room when she repeated it back to me from my own notes.

" 'To choose one's attitude in any given set of circumstances, to choose one's own way.' What does that even mean?" she'd asked. And then, "Why should I care what this guy thinks?"

Why should you care? The man survived the Holocaust. That's what I should have said. But then she peeled off her top, and she wasn't wearing a bra beneath her itchy Fair Isle sweater, so I didn't say anything.

The bathroom line was shorter now. Some had given up, dropped out, and I was the next person waiting. When the door opened I looked at the yellow paper one last time.

"You going?" the girl behind me barked. " 'Cause I'm gonna go if you're not going."

"I'm going," I said. But first I ripped away one of the phone numbers.

Maybe, for at least a couple of months, I could choose my own way.

CHAPTER TWO

I was Joe, and I was from Michigan.

The boat captain and owner of the fish company, Eddie Delgado, didn't ask where in Michigan I was from, but I was so nervous I couldn't stop myself from crafting a long-winded explanation, a story I'd concocted the night before. I said I was out in Greenport getting work with my dad as a plumber and wanted some extra money. He wrote down my name and asked me about my experience, and I said some Great Lakes and deep-sea stuff in the South Atlantic. From the smile in his eyes I could tell he thought I was a bullshitter, but he didn't care because he needed more bodies. I was a young, able body who appeared willing to take direction.

Eddie was this kind-looking man with a nose in the shape of a fishhook and a tattoo of a large-breasted mermaid on his left bicep. When he coughed the mermaid's breasts shook like she was doing a burlesque show. He explained that he sent five boats out every day and he liked to send his guys out in pairs.

"My own boys used to captain the boats, but they went and followed their own goddamn dreams," Eddie explained with a father's proud smile. "One's a manager at that fancy club in the city, the Lime something. The other's going to school for hairdressing.

He's very good. He's worked on the sets of a couple of big TV shows . . . trimming bangs and whatever."

I nodded. "I'm sure he's great at what he does."

"He is. He met Cher last year."

Eddie told me he'd send me out to catch everything from lobsters to porgies to scallops and crabs. I'd get $400 a week. He'd come with me to start, to show me the ropes.

"And you take some fish home," Eddie added. "I'm not promising what you'll get, but you'll get something, and maybe some crabs too, if we have a good week. It's been hell trying to keep up with the demand across the bay and on Shelter. All them rich folks want their seafood pulled right out of the ocean that morning, and we can't get it over there fast enough. I hear some of them are even eating it raw these days." He made a face as if he'd just swallowed a pile of shit. "To each his own. If I'm paying someone to make me fish they'd better take the time to be cooking it."

We didn't go much past Orient Point that first day. "You fucking suck at this job," Eddie warbled out the edge of his mouth two hours later, managing to insult me while keeping a lit cigarette between his lips.

Eddie steered the boat, a forty-foot Hatteras named the *Bailout*, into a section of the bay called Plum Gut where he was insistent that a buddy of his once caught a record-breaking eighty-pound striped bass. Eddie had about fifty different rods on the boat and ten buckets of eels, live bait. It was my job to get the eels on the hook. I'd never seen an eel, much less touched one. The sky was a dull gray, and Eddie said that meant the stripers would be hungry and they liked their eels with a little fight in them. I just nodded, taking it all in, wishing I could write down notes and knowing I couldn't because that would make me look like an idiot.

The one and only time Dad and I went fishing together we caught a bull mahi-mahi, a forty-pounder. It sounded impressive, but we'd paid a pretty penny to be able to do it. Captain Jack, the fisherman we had hired to take us out off Islamorada, about eighty miles north of Key West, called the fish a mother-thumper, and once we hooked it, Jack and his guys stepped in to reel it onto the deck. They heaved the thing into our arms as it fought for its life. Then they took our picture and promptly removed it from our grasp and threw it back into the sea.

My dad still has that photo in his office. In it I'm eleven and my hands and feet are too big for my body. I'm not wearing a shirt, and my chest caves inward. My eyes are closed, but my mouth is open, which is strange because I had braces and I hated smiling with my mouth open for three whole years. The sunlight glinted off the metal in my mouth, sending a beam of white across the photo. I always wished my father didn't keep it on his desk, and yet I was honored that he had a picture of me in his office at all. That's what I'd meant when I told Eddie my experience was in the South Atlantic—a half-day charter.

It's strange that my family doesn't fish. We had been coming out east for as long as I could remember, to a house mere feet from the water. I built a boat. Yet we don't fish. No one I know fishes.

Eddie was right. I sucked at fishing.

Eddie spent most of the morning alternating between telling me I was terrible and singing along to Billy Joel's *The Stranger* on a beat-up portable tape deck. "'Brenda and Eddie were still going steady in the summer of '75,'" he belted out. His wife was named

Brenda, he told me. They used to get a real kick out of this song, thought it meant they were destined to be together.

"Were you?" I asked

Eddie pulled two cans of beer out of the cooler and threw me one. He took a sip and never answered the question.

The first half-dozen eels slipped between my fingers and onto the floor of the boat. Eddie picked them up and threaded the hook right through the lower jaw and out of the eyeball. I forced myself not to look away. I stared right in that eel's beady eye and willed my stomach to stop twisting into retched knots.

"Throw the rest of 'em on some ice for a while," he said. "They're slower when they're cold."

The first time I tried to reel in a fish I got too eager and the line snapped.

"You gotta bring him in slowly." Eddie demonstrated for me on the next one. "Be sweet at first. Treat 'em nice, like a lady. I'd hate to see you on a first date."

Once we'd found our spot and all the equipment was in place Eddie became a well-oiled machine and I became less of a liability. I only had to do what he said.

"Grab that line."

So I did.

"Get me more ice."

So I did.

"Hold that one tight . . . needs a little fight before he comes in. Show him who's the boss." He did that last bit in a wildly accurate imitation of Tony Danza.

I held.

"More eels."

I fetched.

I did absolutely anything Eddie asked me to do. By the end of the morning I could even hook an eel in less than a minute. I'd reeled in a few twenty-pound stripers all on my own.

When we were finished Eddie told me to take the day's log into the office and square everything away with someone named Kit. "She's my daughter," he said. I'd expected Kit to be older than me, given that Eddie looked like he was pushing sixty. But Kit was younger, a petite girl wearing a plain white tank top with sun-kissed blond hair that was cut short and fell right to the middle of her cheekbones. She reminded me of Nicole Diver on the cover of *Tender Is the Night*. They shared the same melancholy look in their eyes and scornful slash of a mouth.

"I was out with your dad today." I announced myself when she didn't look up from a thick handwritten ledger.

"Good for you," she said in response. I didn't know what to say to that, so I just nodded, even though she wasn't looking at me.

"Which boat?" she asked finally.

"The *Bailout*."

Kit finally looked up from the desk, and I was happy to see a small shimmer of surprise flick through her gray eyes, like I wasn't at all what she was expecting to find.

"I'm Joe." I extended my hand before realizing it was still slick with fish guts. Kit knew better, though, and she didn't take the offered hand, merely cocked her head to the side.

"Where are you from, Joe?" she asked with much more skepticism than her father had.

"Michigan," I replied, my voice weaker than I would have liked.

"You don't have an accent."

"People from Michigan don't have an accent." I had no idea if that was true. I wasn't sure if I knew anyone who was actually from Michigan.

"They do. It's a Midwestern kind of thing. And they put an *s* on the end of everything. You sound like you're from right here."

Maybe she was right about Michigan. I tried to think of something halfway decent to explain why I sounded exactly like she did with just a twinge of annoying Ivy League petulance. "I spent a lot of time out here as a kid, with my dad. My parents are divorced so . . . well . . . I'm working for him now. Doing plumbing work."

"Your dad Frank Bianchi?"

"No."

"Abe Schmidt?"

"Nope."

"Those the only two plumbers I know on the North Fork."

"He does a lot of commercial work on the South Fork. Hotels, restaurants." I knew I couldn't keep this parade of lies up much longer. I wasn't built to lie, and I'd told more in the past twenty-four hours than I'd probably told in my entire life.

"You're too pretty to be a plumber." She paused. "Or a fisherman."

"I'll take that as a thinly veiled compliment." Before the words were out of my mouth I knew I'd sounded like some Ivy League preppy, like Ryan O'Neal in *Love Story* or something.

I thought I saw the edges of her mouth twitch toward a smile, but they didn't quite make it there.

Kit finally reached her hand out to shake mine, which was a funny thing to do after we'd already introduced ourselves. I wiped my palms off on my bathing suit before I took it.

She held on to my fingers longer than I expected. "You have very soft hands. Like a princess. Do you rub them with lotion before you go to bed?"

Kit's voice was low like Caroline's but without the patrician accent cultivated by twenty-one years living above Eighty-First Street.

"Lanolin oil, actually. Straight from the sheep's belly."

At least that made her laugh. It was the only true thing I'd told her so far.

"Oh, Joe from Michigan. I am sorry to say it, but I don't think you're gonna last a week on that water."

Kit was finally smiling, and when she smiled it changed her entire face.

"Okay, Kit from Long Island," I said with a sharp grin. "I'll take your bet."

CHAPTER THREE

I needed a nap. Just a small one before I was going to meet Sperry and some of his frat brothers turned bankers for a dinner that would consist of a lot of beer, not very much food, and a lot of talk about IPOs, LBO, and other acronyms I could care less about.

The small spit of beach right before West Neck Point looked like a good place to dock the boat and take a quick breather before continuing across Noyack Bay.

My bones ached with exhaustion. For a week straight I'd risen before the sun was up and crossed the bay, getting to the ship before Eddie to get everything loaded and ready for him. The fatigue felt good maybe because of its novelty. I'd never worked my body, really worked it and used it, for so many hours in a day.

The sand was soft and warm, and within minutes I'd surrendered to sleep.

I don't know how long I was out before I felt a sudden and swift poke in my ribs. When I opened my eyes I saw that the offending poker was a stick of driftwood and the other end was attached to a tall, reedy brunette, her face mostly obscured by large dark sunglasses. Her skin looked almost golden in the sun. Thick, dark hair fell like a cape across her ivory shoulders.

"Ow," I whelped in a way that I immediately recognized as incredibly unattractive.

"What are you doing on my beach?" She spoke with a thick accent, not French, maybe Greek or Italian.

"West Neck is a public beach." I have no idea where I mustered that kind of confidence; perhaps hers was contagious.

She pointed with a long elegant finger. "Starting over there. This beach is mine."

I rubbed my ribs. "It's still not very nice to go around poking people. Even if it is your beach."

"I poked you because I thought you might be dead," the woman said. "You're not dead." She seemed to have no opinion about this conclusion.

"I'm not dead. For some reason." I didn't want her mad at me. "I'm sorry."

The woman's hair covered more of her body than her barely there black bikini, and I was almost embarrassed to look directly at her, but looking away would have been impolite. If I knew how to be anything, it was how to be polite.

"Which house is yours?"

"Right through those trees." She pointed again. "We've rented it for the summer." Despite the accent her pronunciation was impeccable. As she spoke she thrust her shoulders back to give her words even more authority.

"I should head b-b-back," I stuttered slightly. "Thank you for not calling the cops on me."

"You are taking your boat?"

"I am." I looked over at it. *Arabella* was still there. The water was closer to her now, but not dangerously so.

"That could be tricky." She lifted a hand to shield her eyes from the sun and turned toward the horizon. I followed her gaze to find a wall of dark violet thunderheads rushing into the harbor.

"While I'm sure you are an incredibly accomplished sailor, judging by your vessel"—she shot a glance at *Arabella* that conveyed curiosity and concern—"I wouldn't send anyone out in this."

"I'll be okay," I insisted.

"You can come back to my place," she suggested, still gazing out at the weather on the horizon. The storm clouds grew like a quickening bruise.

When I didn't answer straightaway she smiled. "Or you can drown. Your choice." She pivoted on a set of perfectly manicured red toes and walked off in the direction away from the point. I didn't have a choice. I pulled my boat farther up onto land to make sure she was safe and dutifully followed this strange woman like a puppy dog.

"Will your husband mind my coming home with you?" I yelled after her, trying to make her hear me over the wind that had just begun to howl like a banshee.

"Not home. He's in the city. Always in the city. He keeps me here in my beautiful prison."

It turned out that her beautiful prison was a grand old Victorian with a wraparound deck. The floor was rickety and uneven and made a comforting and familiar squeak as I followed her inside. The decor was the same as our house. Mostly white furniture, seashells scattered on every available surface of battered antique, lots of light wood accents, and rugs that didn't look expensive that definitely were expensive. The difference was that her place was a total mess, pillows ripped off the couch and thrown on the floor in front of a fireplace that was surrounded by half-empty bottles of red wine. A deck of cards in the midst of a game of solitaire littered the middle of the foyer. Giant canvases leaned against the walls covered in various states of unfinished paintings.

The more complete pieces could best be described as what would happen if Jackson Pollock and Mark Rothko had a threesome with Georgia O'Keeffe—colorful, loud, confusing, and vaguely erotic.

"I don't even know your name," I said by way of restarting the conversation once we were in the house.

She made no move to straighten up. My seeing her mess clearly had no effect on her. "Elisabetta. But if we become friends you can call me Bette." It was a moment that called for a wink, but there was no wink.

Outside rain pounded against the shutters, and the sky grew dark as night.

Elisabetta. I was fairly certain I would never earn the right to call her Bette, but I knew I wanted to. She picked up what I thought was a throw blanket off the couch, but it turned out to be some kind of complicated shawl that she tied around her neck so that it fell like a dress over her body.

It was only once she removed her sunglasses that I realized she was much older than I had expected. It wasn't any one thing in particular that tipped me off. There were hardly any lines on her face. It was something in her eyes, a haunted expression. She wasn't quite as old as my mother, at least I didn't think so, but she wasn't too far off.

"Drink?" she asked.

"Water would be nice." I was parched.

It wasn't the answer she wanted, and clearly it wasn't one she would accept. "Wine."

"Sure. I guess," I said. I'd never had a drink alone with anyone close to my mother's age, and I didn't drink all that much wine.

"Red."

Again, it wasn't a question.

I searched for somewhere to sit and ended up picking the cushions off the floor and replacing them on the couch. It says something about me that I felt compelled to tidy up, and I'm not sure that I liked what it said. I was patting one cushion down, actually fluffing it like a total loser, when she returned with two empty wineglasses.

"What a good houseboy you are," she said with a beautiful grin.

She picked up one of the half-drunk bottles from next to the fireplace and poured us two glasses nearly to the top. For a moment she looked as though she might fling the empty bottle against the brick of the fireplace, watch it shatter, and then cackle uncontrollably. I was already slightly terrified of her.

But she didn't throw anything. Didn't laugh. Instead, she placed the bottle back down, raised the overflowing glass to her lips, and lapped at it like a cat. She did the same to the second one and handed it to me.

Then she collapsed onto the floor in a heap of coltish legs and arms and sprawled onto the remaining couch cushions.

"Join me." Again, it wasn't a question.

I inched off the sofa like a worm and did as I was told, sitting as far away from her as I possibly could without offending her. *How the hell did I get here? I should leave.* Part of me felt like I did when I was entertaining my mother's friends when they came over for bridge. I'm not bragging or anything, but my mother's friends absolutely adored me. I'd been trained well in the art of making mature women feel seen and appreciated. Deidre made sure of that. It was all about the questions. Never talk about yourself. That's what mother instructed: *You're terribly boring, Henry. I'm sorry, but all teenage boys are. You simply can't help it. Ask them questions about themselves. I promise you no one else ever does.*

"How long have you lived here?" I tried.

"A few weeks." She looked bored. I needed to ask a better question.

"Do you like it?" That wasn't it.

"It is what it is. Why were you on my beach?"

I cleared my throat. "Well, again, it really isn't your—"

"No narration. Just answer my question."

"I was just out in my boat and I wanted to lay down for a few minutes, and I didn't see the storm coming in."

"Isn't checking on the weather the first thing an experienced sailor does before leaving shore?" She laughed, but only to herself.

"Do you sail much?" I asked her to try to turn the attention away from me.

"Never."

Half her glass was already gone. She looked at me more intently. "I just realized I didn't ask you *your* name."

I took a sip of my wine. Who was I going to be to her? My answer would determine much more than I bargained for. I could say Henry Cane and she might recognize the name if she knew a lot of people in my parents' social circle. Then we could play the name game and all that, which might take up enough time that the storm would clear and I could get on my boat and go home.

"I'm Joe."

"Nice to meet ya, Joe." She affected an American accent that made her sound a little like John Wayne crossed with Mr. Rogers. "Where were you coming from that you needed a nap?"

"Just back from work. I do commercial fishing over in Greenport."

Would this impress her? And did I want it to? Why had I even said Joe in the first place?

"A man who works with his hands." She didn't look down to examine my hands the way Kit had. I almost wished she had. After a week on the job she would have noticed virgin calluses and a half centimeter of dirt and blood beneath my ragged nails. I was proud of the way my hands looked now.

"What do you catch here?"

"Striped bass, crabs. Pulled in some scallops today." At least all of that was true, and telling the truth relaxed me enough that I took a long sip of the wine.

"Mmmmmmm," she murmured. "I adore scallops. Do you want me to tell you how I make them?"

I nodded, rapt. Of course I wanted to know how this woman made scallops.

"I let them sit overnight slathered in butter. Now, Joe. I'm not talking about that shit you call butter in this country. Real butter . . . the kind that's filled with fat and salt. Then the butter seeps into their little bodies, infiltrating every hole and pore, tickling their insides." I swear she licked her lips when she said that. Not in an obvious way, but just the tip of her tongue rolling over the tops of her bottom teeth as if she could taste what was about to happen next.

"The next day I throw them on the piping-hot pan for just a minute on each side. No more or you'll destroy them. Then . . . more butter."

I could probably have listened to her talk about butter for the rest of my life.

"Joe, Joe, Joe." She sang my name while swirling the last bit of wine around in her glass. I wondered if I should get up and pluck another of the bottles from the floor? But, what if I selected the wrong one, one that she hated. I briefly wondered who had been there before me . . . who had she chosen not to finish all these bottles of wine with? Was this woman in the habit of inviting strange men into her home in the middle of the day?

She seemed to read my mind, or part of it. "Pick a bottle. Any bottle. They're all good. All expensive."

"Why are all the bottles half-empty?" I decided to ask.

"I'm indecisive," she said decisively.

I wandered around the detritus on the floor, finally selecting a bottle of Chianti with a panther or a jaguar baring its teeth on the label.

"I brought that one from home."

"Where's home?" I poured her glass first, filling it nearly to the top, exactly the way she seemed to like it.

"Rome . . . but before that Corigliano Calabro."

The two words sounded quite beautiful coming out of her mouth, but I had no idea where she was talking about. Italy, but where? I nearly admitted to studying in Rome right then, but Joe had never been out of the country, I decided in that moment. He didn't even have a passport. He wasn't even sure how to get a passport. Besides, my study abroad semester never felt like leaving the country. Sure we visited the Colosseum and we biked past the Spanish Steps on our way to class, but we rarely hung out with any actual Italians. Most of our nights were spent at an Irish pub in a hostel popular with expats and exchange students. Since Caroline was spending the same semester in London I was on a train across the continent every other weekend. I never learned much more Italian than how to find the toilet and how to order a decent bowl of pasta in a mid-priced restaurant.

"Where is that?"

"In the toe of the boot of Italia. You wouldn't have heard of it. No one has. Those bastards up in the north say we can't grow a proper Chianti in the south, but they all have their heads up their asses. And with their heads up their asses how could they smell a good wine, much less taste it?"

Usually girls cursing was kind of a turnoff for me. Or maybe it wasn't. Maybe I just hadn't heard the right girls curse, because I was captivated with the way Elisabetta used foul language.

"I've never been to Italy," I lied.

She cocked her head to the side. "You might like it. You might not. It isn't for everyone. People like to go on and on about how Italy is *soooooo* beautiful. But everywhere is beautiful if you want it to be. Italy is very poor and very rich and very happy and very sad. But no one ever says that." She crossed and uncrossed her legs, shifting the material on her shawl so that it rode up high on her ivory thigh. She made no move to push it back down her leg.

"How'd you end up in Rome?"

Her lips shifted slightly to the right, and she bit down on the bottom one. Then her eyes darted left and right as if she were scanning her brain for the right way to tell the story. "See, one day I was in the market and I saw an American man there. He was fat and with his wife and she was quite pretty with expensive shoes, nice purse, so he didn't seem like much of a threat when he walked over and started talking to me. He started speaking to me in English very slowly and very loud. I didn't speak English but my friend Angelo did. He translated for me. The man said he was a modeling scout for the Ford agency and he liked the way I looked and he wanted me to come to Paris to take some photos with him. I thought he was kidding, and I laughed and laughed and left him in the market because I had to get home. My parents were expecting me for dinner." Her eyes sparkled a little when she talked about the little town and her family. They were dark brown, almost black, and fringed with eyelashes so long they resembled a Japanese fan.

"How old were you?" I was trying my hardest to focus on her face and not the expanse of bare thigh that grew just a little every time she became more animated in her conversation and flailed her hands busily through the air.

"Fourteen."

"You were a child."

"I was a grown woman by then." My statement seemed to ir-ritate her. She stared hard at me from top to bottom.

"Women mature faster than men. *You*," she began, and then sipped her wine, "are still a child."

How did she know how old I was? Part of me wanted to defend myself. Child? I'd just graduated from Princeton. In two months I would be the second-in-command at the largest independent publishing house in New York City. But I didn't. Joe wasn't any of those things. And besides, I knew she wasn't entirely wrong.

I prodded her to keep going. "So what happened?"

"The fat American man showed up at my parents' house the next night just as we were about to sit down to dinner, which meant we had to invite him in because to not invite him in would have been very, very rude. My parents, they didn't speak English either—to be honest they barely even wrote Italian—so we had to call Angelo over from down the street. He translated, and the man had a check for me for five thousand dollars. That was more than my parents made in a year. I didn't like the look of that man, but I didn't hate it either. I went with him to Paris on the condition that Angelo come with me."

"Was Angelo your boyfriend?"

"No. No. Angelo is queer. He does windows at Barneys now. That's one of the reasons I agreed to go to Paris. He needed to leave more than me. If he'd stayed another year they would have made him marry the cross-eyed girl with the limp who lived over the hill. I loved him and needed to protect him, so he came with me, and the rest is history. They took my pictures for a little while, and now I am here in this prison on the beach in New York."

I could tell there was an entire chunk of the story she was purposely leaving out, more than twenty years, but I didn't press her.

"It's a beautiful prison," I tried.

"Soooooooo beautiful." She was mocking me.

"That's quite a story."

"It is a story," she replied matter-of-factly. "Now. Do you need to eat food?"

I glanced out the window. The rain and the wind were only growing stronger, but I'd been inside for a little over an hour and didn't want to overstay my welcome.

"It will be like this for a while. I can tell. I always know when a storm is coming and when one is staying and when one is ready to die."

"How would you know that?"

"I'm a witch." She stood then and strode into the kitchen. The thing that she'd tied around herself left her back entirely bare to within a centimeter of the curve of her backside.

As soon as she walked away I stood to follow her, already a little wobbly from the wine. I reached out to place my hand on the small of her back, but pulled it away at the last second. I lingered in the kitchen and waited for a command because my mother raised a son who knew to always walk into a kitchen and ask if he could do anything to help even if the answer was nearly always no.

Elisabetta was already bent over at the waist, rummaging around in the fridge. As I took in her perfect figure I considered turning around and walking out of the kitchen and the front door right then because for the first time since she found me on the beach I had a hint of what could happen if I stayed.

"Why waste time with cooking?" she asked, turning away from the fridge with her arms full. "Shall we have a dinner of cheese and meats and whatever is in these jars here and, oh, some nuts. Maybe some nuts. How does that sound?"

I smiled at her because it did sound delicious. "That sounds good. At least let me get some plates, napkins . . . a knife or two."

She pointed me in the direction of silverware and a wooden cheese board, and we managed quite a nice spread. When we returned to the living room Elisabetta placed the food in front of the fire and immediately poured us two more glasses of wine.

"Is your husband coming home tonight?" I couldn't imagine the answer would be yes, unless he was inclined to finding his wife sprawled on their floor with strange men.

She waved her hand in the air.

"No. Maybe this weekend. Maybe not."

"What does he do?" I asked the question with genuine curiosity about what kind of job would keep a man so easily from a woman like this one.

"What does any man really do?" She narrowed her eyes in a playful way. "What do you do, Joe?"

"I fish," I said. "Remember?"

"And?"

"And that's it."

"Is your father a fisherman?"

Before I could answer I felt her nudge me with a toe. This nudge was the exact opposite of the poke on the beach. It was gentle, almost inviting. It started at my ankle. Then she ran her big toe slowly up my calf and stopped there, retracting her foot and returning it to rest on top of the other foot as if it had never happened.

"He's a plumber," I said, because I had to say something. I rolled from my side to my stomach hoping she wouldn't understand how excited her unexpected touch had made me, how it had sent a shiver up the inside of my leg. "Rich people's houses. Like this one."

"That's honest work." She seemed to approve. "My father was a cobbler. He sewed and nailed shoes together for a living, thousands of shoes that walked thousands of miles."

I kept going. "My dad's a real good guy. Plays the guitar. A lot of Jimmy Buffett. Does open-mic nights all around." I was drunk. In that moment I knew I was drunk because I became a storyteller. Instead of fighting it I let myself enjoy it, telling tall tales about old Joe Senior. He once fought off a crew of about five men who told him he was a piss-poor guitar player. He built my childhood house by hand. He raced cars on Sundays instead of going to church. Joe Senior was the hero of his own goddamn story.

It was hard to tell whether Elisabetta was rapt or bored, but despite the fact that she was clearly outdrinking me she didn't appear drunk.

"He reminds me of someone I know," she said.

"Who?"

"Just someone." She refused to say any more.

"You're a painter," I said, indicating the canvases.

"I play with paint. When do you get to call yourself a painter? Or an artist? Do I need to sell them to call myself a painter?"

"Have you sold anything?"

"Some things."

She rolled over onto her back and pointed at the nearest canvas, an orange-and-red beautiful disaster.

"What does that look like to you?"

I almost said exactly what my wine-addled brain thought it looked like: a vagina engulfed in flames. But it didn't matter how much wine I had had. I knew better.

"Terror?" I said. It was a question. I definitely phrased it as a question.

At least she didn't roll her eyes.

"Are you afraid of it, Joe?"

The honest answer was yes . . . a little. "Maybe I need more wine," I said as a way of not answering her.

"Basement. Come."

My father had always been something of a wine collector. He didn't drink very much of it, but he liked to buy it and show it off and pour it for other people. So I knew a good wine cellar when I saw one, and this one put my father's to shame.

She wasted no time in selecting two bottles and then ordering me to do the same even though I knew there was no way I could possibly consume even another bottle of wine without falling asleep, or worse. I brought them upstairs anyway, and we resumed our spaces in front of the fire. The firelight danced across her face. She was clearly a woman well aware of her beauty and exactly how to use it.

I wanted to reach across the space between us and touch her, or give her some reason to touch me. I had never been the type to make the first move. The realization of that felt pathetic, weak. I could correct it. I could change it right now. Elisabetta was humming softly to herself, a tune that sounded familiar, but I couldn't quite place it. Instead, I looked at my watch.

When she noticed me doing it I flushed with shame.

"I should get back."

"In the dark? Drunk as the town simpleton?"

"I've done it before."

The rain had slowed but not stopped entirely. I needed to get into that boat.

Her wineglass was empty. Mine was more than half full. She took it from my hands and raised it to her own lips, allowing her tongue to run slowly over the ridge of the glass before tipping her head back and letting the remains of the liquid slide down her throat in a single gulp.

"If you must leave I can find you a flashlight . . . maybe a rain jacket."

She stood and stepped over my prone body. All I could do was stare up and marvel at her. She reached a hand down to help me stand. I wobbled but eventually made it into a semblance of an upright position. Our faces were mere inches apart, and I could smell the wine and the spice from the meats in her mouth and something sweet like oranges in her hair. We stayed like that for a brief moment that felt much longer. My heart pounded so hard I imagined my ribs fluttering like the sails of a boat fighting a gale. Heat rose in my cheeks, and I knew I was blushing but had no idea how to stop it.

"You want to leave?" She pursed her lips together and feigned the voice of a child pouting for another cup of ice cream. She moved just an inch closer.

"I should."

Her head tilted forward ever so slightly so that when she spoke again her lips brushed lightly against mine.

"But you don't want to." Again, it wasn't a question. "What do you *want*, Joe?"

It was me who closed the final distance. I know that it was me. I want to believe that it was me. But it was her who wound her fingers around the back of my neck and into my hair and opened her mouth so that when my lips met hers she was ready to completely devour me. Her fingernails scratched at my scalp as she got a grip on my hair, yanking it away from my skin. No one had ever pulled my hair before, and I had no idea how much I'd enjoy it, how it would send waves of pleasure through my entire body.

I groaned as she pressed her body into me. I'd been paralyzed, but suddenly I knew how to move my hands again. I reached my arms around her to grasp her backside, squeezing it, letting my fingers slide down over the firm ridge, lifting her slightly.

I couldn't help but think of her husband, of the damage I was capable of inflicting—but it was a fleeting thought. It was difficult to think about much of anything. I wanted this to happen, but I was also terrified. Caroline and Annie had been girls, as inexperienced as I had been when I went to bed with them. This was different. Elisabetta was a woman. She'd probably been with a lot of men. A lot of different kinds of men. By now she knew exactly what she liked and what she didn't like, and I had no idea if I could do what she needed.

It didn't matter. She was going to take the lead.

"Where do you want to fuck me, Joe?" she whispered, her breath hot in my ear, her tongue flicking along my earlobe as her hand moved slowly down my side and under my shirt, scratching me so hard she may have drawn blood.

I drew back; maybe I flinched. She had this wide-eyed look on her face, innocent almost, as if she hadn't just said the dirtiest thing I'd ever heard come out of a woman's mouth.

"Tell me where in the house you'd like to fuck me."

Is that what I wanted? This had started out like some kind of game, but now it was all too real. And so I went mute.

Elisabetta was an object in motion, and even the most ignorant first-year physics student knows that an object in motion will stay in motion. With a single swift yank my bathing suit was at my ankles.

That's when she took a step back to examine me for a minute that was much longer than comfortable. I let her do it. What else could I do? Every nerve in my body thrummed like a guitar string.

Without warning she dropped to her knees. First she reached over for the bottle of wine and took an incredibly long sip, her head tilted up toward the ceiling, exposing the fine lines running down her neck. She handed me the bottle, and I took it from her because it was the polite thing to do, and I had a sip because I suddenly felt a very strong desire to be even drunker.

She leaned forward, slightly at first and then farther, and looked up at me with a teasing smile playing her lips. I wasn't ready for it when she gripped me hard and adjusted things so that just the tip of me was past her lips. She gave them a whisper-light flutter, commanding and gentle at the same time.

"Oh, oh, oh my God." I didn't mean to say that. It just came out.

Every muscle in my body tensed for what came next, but what came next was absolutely nothing. She stayed like that, her lips resting gently around me, letting her tongue loll about lazily. I thought about all the things I should be doing, or not doing. I could grasp her hair, pull her into me. But I didn't do anything. I simply waited.

When she pulled back and leaned on her haunches to take another sip of wine I wondered exactly how long I could continue waiting, how long I could keep from completely embarrassing myself. I'd drank so much wine. How long could I even stay hard, even for a woman like this?

When she came back to me she drew me deeper into her mouth. It was warm and sticky from the wine.

I was close.

She knew it.

Right before I couldn't hold it back any longer she stood and stepped away from me again. She reached one hand behind her neck and released both the shawl and the bikini top beneath it in a single twitch of her fingers, like a snap. The fabric dangled from her fingers.

Her bare breasts were the most beautiful things I had ever seen.

I reached over to cup one in my hand, and when I squeezed it ever so slightly she laughed.

"Are you testing a melon? Maybe an avocado? Am I ripe?" She let the *p* sound in *ripe* pop in the air.

She moved my hand back to my side. "I will show you how I like to be touched." Her boldness and self-determination loosened something in me. It could have been the booze too, but mostly it was her. Just knowing that she was going to tell me exactly what she wanted made me believe that maybe I could give it to her.

Slowly she peeled down her bottoms and stood in front of me, daring me to examine her the way that she had considered me. I could hardly remember how to breathe. If someone had asked me to describe the perfect woman I wouldn't have even been able to describe her, because I never would have imagined that she could have actually existed.

She was unshaved, unwaxed, her pubic hair a wild and unruly thing, completely different from the cutesy shapes of both Annie's and Caroline's, a landing strip, a heart, once an ill-chosen puppy dog that looked more like the state of Wisconsin.

She grasped my hand. "Upstairs."

"Stop," I managed to murmur, my breath still ragged and strange. "Can I just look at you? For another minute."

Maybe she thought that was sweet, because she indulged me, standing there, letting me admire her.

Then she led me into a room that clearly wasn't the master but wasn't small either. It contained a king-size bed, perfectly made and covered in what seemed like a hundred pillows. At least half of them went flying onto the floor when Elisabetta shoved me hard on the bed. She held her makeshift dress in her right hand. It dangled like a flayed snake.

I'd never felt so exposed and so completely seen as I did in that moment.

"Hands over your head," she ordered.

I did as she said because what other choice did I have?

"That's it. Now. Stay."

She cracked the piece of flimsy fabric in the air like an insane lion tamer. In a single swift move she straddled me, her hands working the cloth around my wrists, binding them over my head, effectively rendering me immobile.

The knots were tight but not so tight they'd cut off my circulation. I couldn't help but think she'd make an excellent second mate on a sailboat. The hardest part is always getting someone to tie the knots correctly.

"Oh, Joe." She looked down at me and her smile curled into something beautiful and sinister. "Now you're all mine. Whatever am I going to do with you?"

CHAPTER FOUR

"Jesus Christ, kid. You're a worse disaster than usual." Eddie grabbed the eel from my hand.

"The eye and the mouth. Eye and the mouth. It ain't rocket science. You don't need a Princeton degree or anything. You put da hook into the mouth and you bring it out da eye."

"Sorry, Eddie."

I poured him some more coffee from his thermos just to do something helpful and smelled a whiff of whiskey alongside the Folgers. He must have noticed that I noticed.

"The best part of waking up," he cackled.

He was right. I was a disaster that morning. I couldn't think or even see straight. You know that saying about someone screwing your brains out? That never made any sense to me. In fact, it was one of those phrases that irritated me exactly because it didn't make any sense. I liked my similes and metaphors to be orderly.

But now I understood. I was stupid with lust and also spent in a way I'd never been spent before. Elisabetta was insatiable. When I thought it was time to rest, to finally get some sleep, she wanted more, and she knew exactly how she wanted it, and it was different every time. It was nearly dawn when she'd finally had enough of me, and she made that clear by kissing me hard on the lips and then rolling over and falling immediately asleep, gently snoring like a tiny kitten.

Sleep was not an option for me, no matter how exhausted my mind and body may have been. I waited an hour, just until the sun crept over the horizon, and I limped out of the room. The downstairs looked like it was struck by an earthquake or tsunami.

There wasn't a single clean glass in the kitchen. I put my mouth under the faucet and drank from the tap like a goddamn animal. How that was better than simply drinking from a dirty glass I had no idea. I began opening and closing cabinets, praying I'd find some ibuprofen or Tylenol. It was probably upstairs, but I wasn't ready to go back up there. What the hell would happen if I went back up there?

I forced myself to suck it up and, after locating my bathing suit and shirt, walked out the front door. I shivered in the cool morning air and said a silent prayer that my boat hadn't been washed away the night before.

Thankfully *Arabella* was exactly where I'd left her, but she was filled with about five inches of water. I tipped her over and dragged her down to the water, looking in either direction, trying to decide which way to go. There wouldn't be enough time to head home and clean up, and there wasn't even a real reason to. Instead, I left the boat for the moment and walked out into the bay, dunking my head and then allowing the luxury of floating there for a few minutes, letting the night before wash off me.

A bay bath. I had a nanny who called it that when I was little, real little. My mother chastised her for it, maybe even fired her over it, thinking she was being lazy for not just putting me in the tub. In hindsight I think she was being the opposite of lazy. I think she was just fostering a joy of delight and whimsy and being in the ocean. Deidre hated whimsy.

Sufficiently scrubbed with salt and sand, I headed in the opposite direction of my house and met Eddie on the dock in Greenport.

"You look like something ate you up and then shit you out, kid," he said.

"Something like that."

"I hope she didn't bite." He laughed.

Actually she did bite. And she scratched and pinched, and I had no idea what kinds of marks were still hiding in plain sight up and down my body. I didn't really want to talk about it. I never talked about sex. Not with anyone. Not even Sperry, not details anyway. I just rolled my eyes and shrugged my shoulders.

My hangover really started to show once I tried to bait the lines. I was breathing too fast. I may have even been shaking. I hated myself for that, for being such a wimp. *Be a man. Get it together.* For some reason I heard it in my father's voice even though that wasn't the kind of thing my father would ever say. It was the kind of thing *Joe's* father would say.

Thinking about my father made me go hot with shame. Everything that had happened the night before had been a terrible idea. I'd slept with another man's wife. It didn't matter that the man was a complete stranger; I'd done an awful and unforgivable thing. Polite, well-raised, articulate Henry Cane was a home-wrecker.

"I need something for my headache," I finally admitted to Eddie. He nodded and handed me his thermos and a little white pill that he pulled from his back pocket.

"Mix these together. Should do the trick."

I never believed in the hair of the dog. Sperry swore by it. So did my college roommate Grayson. For Grayson it was always a light beer. He was from Milwaukee, the scion of an old manufacturing family that made some little widgets that allowed other widgets in big machines to do their jobs, so he kept a case of Hamm's under his bed. He said cheap beer kept him grounded. It was a very ungrounded thing to say.

But I took the pill and the drink and sat down on my ass until they started to work. Eddie gave me approximately five minutes to do nothing. "Hey, kiddo, I need some help with this one. She's a monster. I think we got ourselves a monster." His biceps shuddered and twitched as he tried to pull in whatever was on the other end of the line.

"What do I do?"

"Stand behind me. Arms around my waist. I'll brace myself against ya."

He was shaking so damn hard I was convinced the fish would give up and Eddie would come flying backward and crush me. That was the more intimidating proposition than wrapping my arms around the large man's waist and hugging him like a child clinging to an inattentive parent.

We stood like that for five minutes, maybe more. I anchored him and held on for dear life as Eddie pulled with all his might. I squeezed my eyes shut because otherwise I'd be looking at Eddie's intricate origami of armpit hair. But with my eyes closed, a scene from the night before flashed across my mind: Elisabetta on top of me, my hands clasped on the sharp corners of her hip bones as she pushed me deeper and deeper inside of her. *Stop it*, I admonished myself. The last thing I needed was a boner while clutching my massive fishing partner from behind.

With the last final yank on the line I couldn't hold on any longer and I went toppling backward, my head slamming into the deck as Eddie pulled the fish on board.

She was out of the water, still flopping and fighting, a wild thing, the sun glinting all the colors of the rainbow off her silvery scales. We were eye to wobbly eye. I stared dumbly at the once mighty, now pathetic thing. A sticky mess of blood leaked from the back of my head.

"You know how many filets that thing is gonna make?" Eddie's voice sounded far away. I didn't know. I had no idea what the answer was.

The fish and I blinked at each other and then we both closed our eyes and passed out.

The bass weighed in at fifty pounds. Not a record, but nothing to sneeze at either. Although Kit didn't even sneeze or offer a "good job, buddies."

"Hey, Kitty Kat, you got a first aid kit? Joe got banged up pretty bad hauling this one in," Eddie said.

"In the back closet. There's supposed to be one on every boat." Her nose was buried in the ledger.

"That's your job, not mine, sweetheart."

She finally looked at me. "You look like shit. A fish did that to you?"

I rubbed at the back of my head.

"He had a rough night, Kitty Kat," Eddie answered before I could stop him. "Didn't ya, Joe?"

I started to mumble something, but Kit had already rolled her eyes at her dad's explanation.

"Be careful out there" is all she said. "You break your neck or your head or your ass, well, that's on you."

Eddie emerged with a first aid box and made me sit on the chair next to Kit while he swabbed at the back of my head with some paper towels covered in hydrogen peroxide.

"He's gonna live. Don't you worry."

To my surprise Kit smiled then. When her mouth opened I noticed that her top front teeth overlapped each other slightly and she had a deep dimple in her right cheek.

"You shoulda been a surgeon, Dad," Kit said dryly. "The world weeps at losing your talents to the sea." She rooted around in the first aid kit until she found a bottle of aspirin. She shook two chalky white pills into my outstretched hand. "'The progress of rivers to the ocean is not so rapid as that of man to error.'"

The turn of phrase surprised me. I knew it instantly. "Voltaire," I said.

Kit looked at me hard then, and I tried to dial it back. Joe, the son of a plumber, the wayward fisherman, shouldn't so quickly identify an obscure quote from one of the philosophers of the early Enlightenment.

"Or maybe I heard it on Oprah."

There was no way around it. I'd revealed something I hadn't meant to. I'd made a mistake, a big one.

CHAPTER FIVE

"I'm wearing women's underwear," Sperry whispered in a voice that was slightly louder than a whisper, as if maybe he wanted someone other than me to hear it too.

What was the right response to that? Surprise? Curiosity? Non-chalance?

I went with a combination of the three.

"Oh! Really. Whose?"

"Posie Montague's. She told me if I wore them all night she might come home with me."

I dialed up the curiosity. "What kind of underwear?"

"The flossy kind. Just a string in my ass, bro. And here's the thing." He finally lowered his voice to an actual whisper. "I kind of like it."

Benefit season. Most people I know lived for the damn things. And Whole Love, the white-tie soiree where Sperry was wearing Posie Montague's thong, was the summer's premier benefit, at least according to the people who ranked such things. Around here, a lot of people ranked such things.

Whole Love was always held at this big-name fashion designer's house out on billionaire row in Southampton Village. It was the kind of place you would expect a high-end fashion designer to live in, all modern lines and glass and steel beams. My mother and her friends hated everything about it, but they never told the high-end fashion designer that. There had been another house on the property when he bought it, a big old mansion that had been there for a hundred years, but even though it was supposed to be protected by the local historical society, he paid enough money to the right historian to get it razed to the ground. The guy was crazy rich like that and crazy famous. He was like household-name famous. Even I had heard of him. In fact, the underwear riding up Sperry's ass at that very moment may have been made by that guy, or at least some factory he owned in China.

Palm trees populated the backyard. *Palm* trees, real ones. They were planted there every summer, and in the winter they would be returned to a greenhouse in Hampton Bays. Their relocation and storage costs were something over a million a year.

Whole Love was very serious about being white-tie. White-tie is the same as black-tie but white, and all the women wear white gowns, except in recent years some had taken to wearing their own white tuxedos with nothing underneath the top except maybe a flimsy white bra. I wore a white tuxedo, picked out for me by Mother and delivered that morning. Refusing to wear a bow tie had been the only decision of my own I made regarding the event. Once I returned to being Henry I couldn't help but be the ever-obedient son, even with my mother more than three thousand miles away.

Mother was on the board of Whole Love, had been forever, and that meant she bought a table every year and filled it with my father's writers, many of whom we hosted for the entire weekend. We would fly them in from place like Driggs, Idaho, and Cloudcroft, New Mexico, and Los Angeles, a city Deidre despised and had avoided for all her forty-five years. These were big-deal writers, National Book Award winners, a Pulitzer finalist. But they all swooned when they got to the Hamptons and saw a celebrity who was on some sitcom like ten years ago. I didn't get it, and I didn't pretend to. Maybe I didn't watch enough television or read the right magazines, but I couldn't tell you the difference between George Clooney and George Harrison, both of whom were rumored to be in attendance that evening.

This year Mother bought the table before she knew about going to Paris, and she didn't trust me to chaperone any of Father's writers, so she told me I was mature enough to invite my own friends.

"Not Brett, though."

"Of course not, Mother."

Fat chance. That would have been impossible. It was a big table, and the second Sperry knew I had it he took over the seating arrangements, and besides, he was better at inviting people anyway. Still, from the moment I walked through the white check-in tent and out to the sprawling emerald-green lawn I was an object of curiosity because folks thought I had some famous writer in my care when all I had was Sperry, a doughy former college athlete wearing women's underwear.

Posie came over and kissed me on the cheek. Posie was beautiful in a very particular way. Sperry once described it as a look of perpetual walk of shame with her forever-smudged mascara and disheveled bottle-blond bob. "She's like Courtney Love without the danger," he'd said. "Like I don't necessarily think she's going to kill me, but it wouldn't surprise me, and I might like it." I wondered if Posie had recently taken off the underwear she'd given Sperry to wear and if that meant she wasn't wearing anything at all beneath the white lace cocktail dress that looked like a sexy doily. Thinking about Posie's undergarments made me think about Elisabetta. To be honest I hadn't stopped thinking about Elisabetta since I left her house more than a week ago. I had to stop. The thoughts were becoming something of an obsession, and I wasn't the kind of guy who got obsessed about anything.

"Thanks for the invite, Henry," Posie said. It wasn't like her father, the hedge fund mogul Jack Montague, couldn't have bought a table of his own. Posie's dad had been allowed to purchase a $5,000-a-seat table but had been banned from the event this year due to an incident last year where he punched a cater waiter in the face. He cracked the guy right in the jaw. Jack was convinced the young man was sleeping with his wife since he'd found his name tag beneath a bed in the Montague pool house, a five-bedroom structure costing more than what most public school teachers will make in a lifetime. It turned out the poor waiter wasn't sleeping with Mrs. Montague, but he *was* sleeping with Posie's brother, recently home from a year abroad in Barcelona where he was doing a Fulbright. Old Jack Montague was arrested and charged with assault. Of course, nothing stuck after Jack covered all the waiter's bills and some additional reconstructive surgery that landed him a role in a Martin Scorsese movie that started filming in Tribeca last March. The Jack Montagues of the world could punch all the service workers they wished. Everything would always work out in their favor.

Anyway, all that meant was that Posie was grateful to be there without her father. She'd brought along her roommate from Yale, a petite redhead named Sierra who was constantly chewing on her hair. "I was conceived on the Pacific Crest Trail," Sierra said by way of explanation about her name, even though no one asked.

The girls were sipping the night's signature drink, a fiery red concoction that resembled a negroni but wasn't being called a negroni because that would be boring. It was instead called the Mount Fuji. The year's theme seemed to have something to do with a white winter in Japan, fitting for a summer fete, and the host had hired snow monkeys, thankfully accompanied by handlers, to wander the grounds to add some real northern Japanese authenticity. So far they seemed to simply be scowling at guests and stealing crudités from discarded plates.

This year the owner of the house also created a signature scent for the evening. It had been bottled into elaborate crystal containers and would be auctioned off, ten bottles in all, during the live-auction portion of the evening. We were currently in the silent-auction portion of the event, but androgynous dancers, completely nude save for a coat of gold paint, whirled through the yard spritzing the scent in the air to entice the future bidders. When asked to describe the scent, the very famous designer would say only it was the scent of "people helping other people." The crowd ate that up with humble nods, and you could tell they were determined to bid high on bottles of altruism-scented water.

I don't want to sound like some kind of an ungrateful jerk. All of it was for a good cause. Whole Love raises something like five million every summer to feed the homeless in New York, and if it takes some moody snow monkeys and painted dancers with nipples that could cut glass to do that, then I'm all for it.

Sierra offered me a sip of her drink. I refused and said I was going to stick to beer, since I was planning on driving home. She leaned in and whispered in my ear. "I've got Vicodin if you want some." She placed her hand on my waist. It was tiny, like her, and it rested just over my hip bone.

"I think this is the best Whole Love benefit yet," Posie murmured into her cocktail. "And what do you think is in these drinks? They're out of this world."

"Lighter fluid?" Sperry replied. "I'm feeling a little woozy in the best possible way. Hey, Henry, if I black out can you bid on that weekend in Sun Valley for me?"

"Sure thing, buddy." I briefly wondered who else Sperry had invited to our table. I assumed a few guys from high school who I'd spotted across the long expanse of yard that led down to the private beach. We had already nodded in acknowledgment of the others' presence, knowing we'd catch up more properly once we'd all had the appropriate number of drinks. There would probably be a couple more girls, a spare as Sperry would say, in case Posie didn't work out. For a minute I pictured Sperry getting drunk and taking home some other girl, having her unbutton his pants only to find Posie's underwear. For the next moment I desperately wanted that to happen.

Once Posie and Sierra started getting nostalgic for their Yalie days of naked parties and a cappella octets, I wandered off with the loose promise of procuring everyone more drinks and headed in the general direction of the bar. There was a reggae band playing on a platform where the grass stopped and the sand began. Nothing felt very Japanese about that, but it didn't seem to bother anyone. Older men danced with their younger second and third wives, still too sober to truly let loose but tipsy enough to do that old-white-man dance move that just looks like really effusive shrugging.

While I was waiting in line at the bar, one of the painted perfume pushers approached me, and I held up my palms in surrender.

"Don't shoot," I said.

They backed away slowly, making the waggling hand motions of a mime who had failed mime school.

"Henry Cane. Look how tall you've gotten."

I turned around to find Sarah Knowles, my mother's longtime tennis partner and another Whole Love board member. I leaned down to kiss her cheek, slightly rattling the sparkly cat-eye glasses on her nose. She went for the double cheek kiss, which meant she must have just gotten back from somewhere in Europe. The double cheek kiss usually lasted about a month after someone got back from Europe.

"Good to see you, Mrs. Knowles." She wore a gown covered in white crystals that made her shine like a snowflake. It even had a train, like a wedding gown that I imagined must be incredibly disconcerting for the snow monkeys, forced to watch it move across the ground like a disconnected ice floe through a sea of green and well-shod feet.

"Are you in charge of Sam Hartwell for the evening?" Sarah Knowles asked me.

"I'm not sure what you mean."

"Didn't your mother invite Sam Hartwell to this dinner? I assumed that's who'd invited him to give the opening remarks."

Sam Hartwell. Sam Hartwell was somewhere at the party? The man whose first book had made me actually want to work in editing and publishing? The only man who ever made me believe that good literature could truly change your life? Sam Hartwell was currently on these grounds, perhaps being assaulted by primates and spraymongers just like everyone else, and I was only just finding out about it.

"I didn't bring him, Mrs. Knowles," I said, scanning the crowd beyond her shoulder. "He must have been invited by someone else."

She seemed surprised, but her face was incapable of showing that kind of emotion. Even her eyebrows no longer moved. I'd once heard Sarah Knowles tell my mother "aging gracefully was perfectly fine . . . for other people." Mrs. Knowles used to be this big-deal reporter for the *Wall Street Journal* but had since retired, and now she wrote for one of the many local Hamptons rags, a kind of advice column meets society column. Hamptons gossip is always packaged as a society page, which makes it feel less filthy and sordid and acceptable for a former Pulitzer Prize winner to be writing it.

She seemed to feel obliged to tell me everything she knew about Sam Hartwell. "I heard he's been in New York all summer. He usually lives abroad. Not sure where. But allegedly"—she leaned closer—"his agent forced him to stay in the city, locked up in an apartment somewhere in Midtown until he finishes his next novel."

I had a tattered copy of Sam Hartwell's first novel, *Desolation Wilderness*, on my nightstand at home. I'd first read it when I was just thirteen, but even then it had already been in circulation for more than a quarter of a century. I often thumbed through it when I couldn't sleep, rereading familiar passages that somehow had the power to become new again.

"Who's publishing it?" I asked. It was the kind of thing I should know. In less than two months it would be my job to know.

"I don't think anyone, yet. It's not finished. And who knows if it's any good. His last one wasn't very good." Sarah Knowles was being kind. His last novel, which had come out a decade earlier, had been a critical flop, but it had still sold close to a million copies based on Hartwell's notoriety. "That's why I thought he might have come with you. I thought perhaps your father had purchased the book before Hartwell even finished it, or is courting him. It would be a bold move." She lowered her voice to a conspiratorial whisper. "And your father could use a bold move right about now."

Her candidness surprised me.

"Maybe Mr. Hartwell and I will have a discussion about it tonight," I said, doing my best to channel the confidence of my father. Who knows? Maybe we *would* have a discussion about it. I'd spent my entire life talking to editors and writers, but never one I admired quite this much. I scanned the crowd again, but I wasn't sure I would recognize Hartwell. He was a young man, barely out of his twenties, when *Desolation Wilderness* was published. In his author photo he has a thick mop of dark hair and horn-rimmed glasses, a classically handsome jaw. He's standing out in the woods in a too obvious metaphor. But that was more than thirty-five years ago. I had no idea what he looked like now.

"If I see him I'll send him your way," Sarah Knowles said with a wink as she took two ruby-red Mount Fujis from the bartender.

"What exactly is in the Mount Fuji?" I asked when I approached the bar.

"Gin, Campari, and sweet red vermouth."

"So, it's a negroni," I said.

"It's a Mount Fuji."

"I'll take four of those." If I wanted the confidence to approach Sam Hartwell I knew I was going to have to get a little drunker.

By the time I made it back to Sperry and the girls the bells began tinkling to indicate that it was time to stop mingling and take our seats for dinner.

The composition of our table was exactly as I expected. Sperry, Posie, Sierra, our buddy Jake from Collegiate, who was about to start work at NBC News, and his new girlfriend, Kate, whom he met at William & Mary. Kate had a job in fashion. That's all she said, and no one asked anything else. There were the Chalker twins, Digby and Bradford, redheaded scoundrels who could actually drink Sperry under the table. They were both going to grad school at MIT for something involving actual rocket science. Sperry was convinced they were being recruited by the CIA, and he floated this theory every time he got really drunk. "Because they're twins," he would insist. "They're their own double agents."

And then one final surprise—none other than Annie Westover, the girl I'd lost my virginity to. Sperry grinned and glanced at me as Annie sat down. I'd thought she was off in Los Angeles working as a production assistant for Miramax. I had no idea she was in the Hamptons for the summer.

"I'm not out here for the summer," she said from across the table before I even asked. "I'm here for the weekend. We're filming a period piece. They're trying to turn Georgica Pond into the moors of England. It's trickier than you'd think, and absolutely no one is happy about it."

I found the rest of the table less endearing than Sperry did. There was a lot of talk of money and jobs and very little else, which bummed me out because these were people who studied at the very best schools in the country, who traveled the world, seeing places most people only saw on television, and all they could talk about was who was making a fortune at Bear Stearns and who didn't get into the analyst program at Citi.

When our waiter came by with red and white wine and filled our glasses, Sperry demanded a bottle of tequila for the table, and within minutes one appeared. He insisted everyone do shots to loosen up. Having Annie there, thinking about running into Sam Hartwell, talking to Sam Hartwell . . . it all made me want a shot even though I'd officially given them up as a New Year's resolution. I took one and then another one, deciding I'd ditch my car and call a cab like everyone else.

We were about to toast to some ridiculous memory from high school involving a stolen raccoon mascot and someone's Volkswagen when an old man walked across the stage and began tapping the microphone. His breath came out heavy over the loudspeaker. I didn't pay him much attention at first. In fact, no one paid him any attention. He spoke for a few minutes before the very famous fashion designer stood up from his table and walked onto the stage to join him.

"We have come here tonight in honor of Whole Love, New York State's largest nonprofit serving the homeless population. I'd like to start with a moment of silence in gratitude for our own homes," the designer said.

The crowd took the opportunity to bow their heads, examine their pedicures, check their watches to see how much longer until the fun portion of the evening when they got to bid on extravagant vacations, and reflect peacefully on their many homes.

The shrieking howl of a snow monkey in distress pierced the silence, and the very famous fashion designer continued. "Could everyone please be quiet to welcome our very special guest for the evening, Mr. Sam Hartwell."

That man was Sam Hartwell? That tiny old man. I looked harder, and if I squinted enough and took a sip of tequila while I did it I could almost see the young man standing among the redwoods in the black-and-white photo in the book on my night table.

I knew better than anyone that you should never expect a writer to be a good public speaker. In fact, as a rule of thumb, the better the speaker, the worse the writer. Real writers don't want to be famous, and they don't often have an extrovert's toolbox at their disposal. But I had heard plenty of stories about what Sam Hartwell was like in his younger years. In fact, the tales of Hartwell had taken on something of legend. He rode his motorcycle across the country with nothing but a single backpack and a hundred bucks. He once took on an entire bar of good old boys who wouldn't let his black friend sit at the bar and have a drink with him. He'd lived in the wilderness, eating nothing but fish he'd caught himself and squirrels he shot with a BB gun because his real gun had run out of bullets and he couldn't afford any more. This withered man on the stage couldn't possibly be him.

"Don't you love that dude?" Sperry said. "You've got like nine of his books."

"He hasn't written nine books," I said back, trying to listen. "He wrote one great book."

"But it's your favorite."

"Shut up, Sperry. I can't hear him."

Hartwell was saying something about how he had lived on the streets while writing the first draft of *Desolation Wilderness*, how he was young and strong and still barely survived a winter of homelessness in New York City. He said he was always grateful for the people who gave him a little bit of anything, money, food, booze. He thanked Whole Love for all the money they raised to help the people struggling just to make it through another night. His voice was soft but not weak, and he had the cadence of a natural storyteller. The crowd, once buzzing with their tipsy chatter, was now rapt.

"I'm in New York finishing my new novel. As you can probably imagine, I've been working on it for a long time."

The crowd tittered politely.

"You might call it my life's work. I never would have gotten this far if it hadn't been for the kindness of strangers who came along and gave me the help when I needed it. I also wouldn't have made it this far without my wife. She's here tonight," he said, smiling into the crowd. "She's been living out here while I write and edit in Manhattan with my agent. Some of you may have met her already. If you haven't, say hello tonight. She's the reason I do what I do. She's the reason I do anything."

There was a faint *aw* from the audience.

"Thank you. Thank you, my darling Bette."

My blood ran cold.

I followed Sam Hartwell's gaze. The rest of the crowd was just as curious as I was to see what kind of goddess inspired a man like Hartwell. Everyone stood and clapped, staring at the woman Hartwell had motioned toward . . . the woman with the long dark hair.

CHAPTER SIX

I had to get out. There was no other option. I had to leave right away. I was so desperate to see Elisabetta again that I could feel it in every nerve of my body, but not here, not like this. What the hell was I thinking? Not ever. She was Sam Hartwell's goddamned wife, and I could never see that woman ever again. My eyes scanned the backyard searching for egress. It was a straight shot to the side exit that would lead to the winding driveway, where there would doubtlessly be some parking attendant who could call me a taxi.

My heart thrummed against my ribs, and sweat trickled down my back as I stood up and turned in the direction that would get me out of the party.

"Where you going, dildo? Bar?" Sperry asked. "Get me another Fuji." He jiggled his empty glass.

"Bathroom," I said mechanically. I just kept walking.

"Well, go to the bar on your way back."

"Yeah. Yeah. On it," I said, dodging a waiter carrying a tray of a half-dozen plates of baked goat cheese balls smothering a bed of perky arugula.

Then, returning from a trip to the bathroom, Annie appeared

in front of me. She had a sly look in her eye. She flicked her blond hair over her shoulder and stuck her hand on her hip.

"Stalking me?"

Annie had always had the worst timing. Back when we were dating in the eleventh grade she would always call my house just as my mother had sat down to watch *Murder, She Wrote*, Deidre's guilty pleasure and the only thing she'd consider watching on television that wasn't on PBS. The phone would ring, and Mother would sigh, "That girl again." Annie told me she loved me for the first time the day that I'd gotten my wisdom teeth out, and she had been terribly hurt, like really pissed off, when I didn't respond right away. I didn't love her, but it was the kind of thing you almost always said back to a person when they said it to you in high school. My mouth was so swollen I couldn't even mumble a polite "Me too." Even the first time we'd had sex had fallen victim to terrible timing, as Annie didn't realize she was about to get her period. Both of us were so terrified by the aftermath, assuming, as virgins, that I'd broken her insides. We didn't attempt sex again for months. And now here she was, holding me up, delaying my escape.

"I'm heading home," I said to her.

"But the live auction hasn't even started," she said while blocking my way to the exit. As she talked I couldn't stop staring at her nose. It was an entirely different, brand-new nose. Her old nose had this bump right in the middle of it. It made her face interesting. Of course Annie's face was still beautiful—maybe too beautiful, to be honest—but it was no longer interesting, and that made me sad.

"I don't feel great."

"Did you pet one of the snow monkeys?" She was deadly serious. "I'm sure they're chock-full of diseases. Monkeys always are. They're responsible for half the communicable diseases in Uganda."

It was a strange fact for a film-studies major who grew up on East Eighty-Second Street to be able to share off the top of her head and also probably not true.

"I didn't touch the monkey. I'm just tired. I feel a little feverish."

Annie reached her hand up to my forehead like a mother checking on a child's temperature.

"You aren't warm." She moved her hand down to stroke my cheek. "Stubbly. Are you growing a beard?"

"I just forgot to shave for a couple of days."

"Remember that time you tried to grow a beard in the eleventh grade? And I made you shave it."

She didn't make me. She told me that the beard was making my face smell like a hamster, and I shaved it on my own.

She was already a little drunk and moving in closer.

I forced a cough and then another, really putting my all into it, getting some phlegm going in my throat. Annie lived in fear of germs, even those from the common cold and not a depressed monkey. She took a step backward.

"What do you want me to tell everyone?" she asked. "About you leaving?"

"Could you maybe not say anything for a little while?" I asked, softening my gaze, pleading with her. "I don't want anyone worrying about me."

"Whatever you say. Want me to bid on anything for you?"

"Nah. I'm good. And don't let Sperry get too drunk."

She started to walk away and laughed over her shoulder. "Too late for that. It was good to see you, Henry. Let's try to meet up before I fly back to the best coast." The Annie I dated in high school would never say something like that, and it made me even more sad about her.

But at least I was free.

And then I wasn't.

"Joe. Is that you?"

There were at least ten bars at the party, and she chose this particular one right next to my escape route. I knew I could keep walking. *Nope, not Joe. No Joe here. You must be mistaken, ma'am.* The smart thing to do would be to stay silent. But just the sound of her voice made me entirely irrational.

When I turned around, Elisabetta's narrow face was filled with genuine surprise and confusion.

"What are you doing here?"

I could tell her the truth. I wasn't Joe. I wasn't the son of a larger-than-life plumber. I was Henry Cane, son of Maxwell Cane, and I was at this party as a guest just like she was. My mother paid more than $50,000 for the table I was sitting at with a bunch of friends from high school who I didn't really like very much. I lived in Sag Harbor and the Upper East Side. Collegiate, Princeton. I could tell her that in the fall I'd start work at Empirical Press as the deputy publisher, a job I was surely underqualified for, one I didn't even want but was created specifically for me. I could start to gush about her husband and tell her what a huge fan I was. She probably got that all the time and hated it.

I could pretend that what happened at her house never happened at all.

But Sam Hartwell was shopping for a new publisher. Identifying myself now would almost certainly take my father and our house out of the running before we'd even had a chance to get into the race.

"Elisabetta," I said, not unfriendly. I shoved my hands into my pockets so that I could clench my fists, a physical manifestation of channeling Joe. "I'm bartending here. . . . Good to see you. . . . Wish I could chat. But I need to check on the supplies. The liquor. I need to go get more liquor." I stuttered and swallowed hard, trying to force the lump out of my throat.

I needed to move this conversation along before someone who did know who I was came by and blew my cover. I imagined Annie returning or Sarah Knowles tittering over.

What I wanted to say to her was: *You're married to Sam Hartwell. The Sam Hartwell.*

Instead, I said, "Your husband gave a nice speech."

"He deigned me with his presence this weekend," she replied with a roll of her eyes. "And dragged me to this ridiculous party with all these ridiculous people." For the first time since seeing her sitting at her table I noticed that she wasn't wearing white. In fact, she was the only person at the entire party not wearing white. She wore a red dress that plunged in the front, and from what I could tell there was nothing underneath it. I enjoyed her disobedience. She was also barefoot, her toes painted to match her dress and wiggling in the damp grass.

She placed her palm flat against my chest. "So, bartender, can you fix me a drink?"

I eyed the man already standing behind the bar. Would he stop me? I said a silent prayer that the staff at this party had been told to let the guests do whatever the hell they wanted and walked behind the bar.

"Alex told me to come over here," I said to the bartender with authority. He just shrugged.

"What would you like?" I asked Elisabetta.

"A negroni."

"Ahhh, the night's signature cocktail. The Mount Fuji."

She rolled her eyes again. The gesture was so juvenile but also so fitting that it made me like her even more. "I'm pretty sure it is just a negroni. You silly Americans with your themes and your games. Wouldn't it just be easier to donate to the charity? Here. Please take a check. Take my money and don't bother to spend it on monkeys and mimes and canapés."

"Easier. Probably, yeah. But less fun. And who would employ the many snow monkey trainers of Eastern Long Island?"

"Those poor animals. Make it strong. I need to get very drunk this evening." Her accent made everything she said sound like sex.

I made it strong, and I made it quick, spilling some of the Campari over the top of the glass in my haste. It trickled like blood onto the white tablecloth. I handed it to her and stepped out from behind the bar.

"I really do need to unload some more gin from the truck," I said. "It was lovely to see you."

I sidestepped around her and rushed to the exit, not realizing she was following me until I had finally made it past the check-in tents and to the driveway in the front of the house.

"Joe," she called out to me.

I stopped in my tracks.

"Lovely to see me?" She was grinning. "That's all?"

I tried to look apologetic. "I've got to get back to work. I'll get in trouble if I get caught talking to the guests for too long."

She stepped closer and then even closer. Her husband was

right around the corner. Anyone could walk by and see us. But suddenly I wasn't thinking about any of that. Her boldness had begun to wear off on me.

"You'll come see me again," she said.

Her perfect breasts pressed into my chest. Her nipples were hard against the fabric of my shirt. I imagined them against my bare skin, cupping them, squeezing them, moving my mouth down to devour them. I felt myself getting hard against the fly of my tuxedo. So help me, God, I had to get out of there. Elisabetta's hand reached down to stroke the skin on my stomach just beneath the waistband.

"You'll come Monday at five," she said, her breath hot with liquor and intention. She slid her hand under the waistband now, down the fabric of my white tuxedo pants.

"Your husband," I started.

"My husband will be back in the city by tomorrow morning. You will come." It wasn't a question; it never was with her. She pinched me in a place that made me groan. I was frozen by her touch, her stare. We stood like that for about half a minute, then, as quickly as she appeared, she was gone, sashaying back to the tinkling laughter of the party, a smudge of red in a sea of white.

What had I gotten myself into?

Screw the cab. I decided to walk the five miles home. The sun had barely kissed the horizon, and the cool evening breeze helped clear my head. There are no sidewalks on the roads in the Hamptons, so I'm sure everyone thought I was some kind of radical communist for daring to walk along the shoulder, but I liked the small act of defiance.

It took me a couple of hours, but by the time I made it home I knew two things for certain. I would go to see Elisabetta again, and I needed to be the one to publish her husband's book.

CHAPTER SEVEN

To make up for abandoning him at the party I told Sperry he could bring Posie and Sierra to hang by the pool on Sunday afternoon. His stepmom, Kelli-Anne, was hosting a playdate for Sperry's toddler half sister, and she informed him he wasn't allowed in the house for the entire afternoon under any circumstances. Kelli-Anne already had a hard time fitting in with the other preschool mommies, most of whom were second wives, not fifth. There was apparently a difference.

"I can't believe your dad has a toddler," Posie said. "It's sort of gross. Do you think she'll have another one?"

"No way." Sperry shook his head. "She pulled the goalie on him for Melanie. He won't lose that game twice. He got snipped last year." He paused. "But don't, like, tell anyone. I don't think Kelli knows, and she would be pissed."

"I don't want any kids," Sierra announced, placing one of her curls in between her chapped lips and sucking on the end of it. She was wearing plastic glasses that were painted to look like the British Union Jack, and they covered most of her face, so I couldn't tell if she was being serious. "They're just another way for the patriarchy to keep us down."

Posie nodded, but I was pretty sure she didn't agree. "I'm bored," she announced. The way she said it made you want to do something about it.

"You guys could go to the beach," I suggested, selfishly hoping they'd take me up on the suggestion so I could spend the rest of the afternoon rereading *Desolation Wilderness*.

"I can't stand the sand," Posie said. "It gets all up in my everything."

That made me wonder if Sperry was still wearing her underwear.

"We could go to the polo, I guess," Sperry said, sipping something clear out of one of my mother's crystal highball glasses. He poured a little bit of the liquid onto his stomach and let it pool in his belly button.

"It's hot as a biscuit," he said, and then cringed. "It's something I heard Kelli say."

"Polo?" Sierra raised an eyebrow.

"It's a thing," I said. "It started last summer, I think."

"It's so weird out here," Sierra said. "It's like England without the tweed and the little queen. Stuffy much?"

"Yeah," Posie said uncertainly. She'd grown up coming to the Hamptons, same as the rest of us. I never really thought about it as stuffy. This was just the way things were: people dressed up during the day to drink champagne and watch men on horses knock a ball around. I'd come to think of it as baseball for the rich.

"Let's polo," Sperry insisted. "It'll kill some time before the bonfire."

"Can I wear this?" Sierra wrapped her oversize flannel buttondown shirt around her one-piece bathing suit.

"Probably not," I said.

"Definitely not," Sperry said with disgust.

"Are you going to wear that?" Sierra looked at his khaki shorts and turquoise polo shirt.

"Yeah, but I'm a dude. This is my summer uniform. You should put on a dress."

I was worried Sierra might walk over to Sperry and crack him on the side of the head, but she didn't . . . when in Rome and all.

"Can I borrow something from your mom?" she asked me.

"Me too," Posie said. "I don't feel like going back to my place."

Deidre would have rather burned her clothes than have two strange girls rooting around in her closet, but I was just so bad at saying no. Thankfully, Mother had packed most of the nice stuff for Paris, the Chanel and Dior. But there were some sundresses, flowery things, in there. The girls took their time trying stuff on. A box in the corner caught my eye. I'm not sure why; it was just a box, but something made me crawl over to it, past the rows of shoes and purses. I lifted the lid, unsure what to expect but already filled with guilt for opening something that didn't belong to me.

But the contents of the box did belong to me.

I picked up a batch of faded construction paper and read the smudged ink—*Henry and the Giant Toilet Monster*. I'd been seven when I wrote that story about a half crocodile, half shark that lived in the New York City septic system. My first-grade teacher helped me turn it into a "book," and I had a vague recollection of presenting it to my dad on his birthday. I hadn't seen it since, but my mother had kept it for all these years. It wasn't the only one. There were dozens of stories in that box, things I'd written up until high school when I stopped showing stuff to my parents. I wanted nothing more than to read all of it then, to sprawl on the floor of my mother's closet, enveloped in the slight scent of her old perfume and think about the boy who wrote those stories.

"Maybe I'll stay here," I tried as Posie and Sierra finally settled on two dresses that I'd never actually seen my mother wear.

"No way, dildo," Sperry slurred. "I'm already drunk. You're driving."

Everyone else smoked a joint in the car on the way there. I took it when it came my way, but I took only the smallest hit and tried not to inhale. Pot made me paranoid, and I was already anxious. What if Elisabetta was there? Or worse, what if she was there with her husband? I parked and trailed behind the others in the lot, keeping a careful eye out for a tall Italian, but it was a sea of blondes and sunhats. A few of my mother's friends nodded at me; I nodded back and thought about Elisabetta again.

The polo match was played on a pristine field, but some champagne brand was sponsoring the spectator party underneath a big white tent, like the kind you'd put up in the backyard for your second daughter's first wedding. We settled onto fake antique couches perched on real Oriental rugs splayed across the freshly cut grass.

Posie and Sierra wandered off to find a bathroom. I settled on a fainting couch across from a couple of fortysomething women arguing about whether their friend was a Samantha or a Charlotte.

I felt a pair of hands start kneading my shoulders. Sperry. He always did that when he was high, started giving people shoulder massages. A live peacock strutted across the pretend living room, but no one batted an eye.

"Dude. Yessss," Sperry said by way of pulling me out of a semi-drunk daze and up toward the buffet. "They just delivered a fresh batch of oysters. Let's go to the bar. I'm starving."

"Oysters aren't filling. They're like filler," I said. "Something you eat with other food."

"But I'm gonna hook up with Posie later, and the oysters will help keep me going."

"I'm not sure you understand the definition of an aphrodisiac." I went with him anyway. He wasn't kidding: the oysters were just being unloaded from the back of a truck. I looked closer at the writing on the side of the truck, a faded blue cursive—*Delgado's*. Delgado's. *Shit*.

Maybe there were some guys I'd never worked with before, guys who wouldn't recognize me. "Look at that cute little cater waiter." Sperry suddenly whistled. "She's totally my type."

Sure enough, it was Kit unloading crates from the back of the truck and bringing them over to the raw bar. I grabbed Sperry by the elbow and turned the two of us in the opposite direction. "Come on, Sperry, there are plenty of other girls here."

"Stop it, man." Sperry tried to move us back to the seafood.

The last thing I wanted was Sperry talking to Kit. I felt weirdly protective of her. I didn't even want Sperry breathing next to her.

"I want to place a bet," I said.

"You can't bet on polo, dildo."

"Then I think we should check out the horses."

"You hate horses." He was right. What had my mother always said to me? "You're a fearful child, Henry. Horses can smell fear, so you better not let them smell you."

I had no idea if Kit was just delivering the oysters or if she'd be shucking them for the rest of the afternoon. I also knew very well that I couldn't leave because facing the wrath of Sperry for the second time in a weekend would leave me with too big a debt. Besides, I had to keep an eye on Deidre's dresses.

Posie and Sierra were stomping on divots in the middle of the field like they were Julia Roberts in *Pretty Woman*. They tried to wave us over, and I shook my head. I had this vision of Kit watching me tapping my toe down on the pretty neon green grass, and I pretty much just wanted to die on the spot.

"I want to smoke the rest of that joint," I said to Sperry.

"No you don't, man. You hate pot more than you hate equines."

"I do . . ." I looked back at the girls and decided I needed to speak in Sperry's language.

"It might loosen me up. I could see if Sierra might be into me." I swiveled my head like an owl and looked back at Kit diligently unloading the oysters. She wore black pants and a white button-down shirt, the uniform of service workers the world over.

"I smoked the whole thing," Sperry said. "We need to get some more. My guy lives in Bridge, so he's close. But we need to find a phone to call him." Sperry always had a guy, and that guy was always somehow a phone call and a cab ride away.

The girls ran giggling off the field just before the horses stampeded back on.

Someone popped open a champagne bottle the size of a Bentley and for a few minutes the spectators pretended to understand the rules of polo.

"Should we get something else too?" Sperry was warming up to me warming up to the use of illegal substances. "He's got some crazy pills. I took one the other day and I swear I saw Jesus." A bold statement coming from the grandson of Holocaust survivors.

Behind Sperry I saw the Delgado truck backing up over the grass and onto the dirt road leading away from the polo grounds.

I released a breath I hadn't realized I'd been holding. My jaw started to unclench.

"Maybe we shouldn't order the pot after all." I began to move Sperry back to the girls, back to the raw bar.

"You're such a cock tease," he complained. "Or should I say a coke tease."

"We weren't gonna order cocaine, Sper."

"But we could have." He pouted.

"I'm the worst friend in the entire world," I agreed with him. Someone was going to blow my cover. It might be Kit. It could be Elisabetta. It probably wouldn't be Sperry, but there was no way I could keep this up for the entire summer. Keeping Henry and Joe straight was going to give me an aneurism. But then so would the alternative, a typical Hamptons summer. Sperry, pool, bar, club. Sperry, pool, bar, club.

Sperry snapped his fingers in front of my eyes. "Earth to dildo. You're not the worst friend. You, Henry Cane, are the best guy I know."

CHAPTER EIGHT

I couldn't get enough of her.

I craved every single part of her in a way that I had never wanted anything in my entire life. Elisabetta became a habit, a bad one and one that was impossible for me to break. I went to see her on the Monday after the Whole Love benefit and promised myself it'd be the last time. But then there I was, back again on Tuesday and Wednesday and Thursday. I saw her four times a week for three weeks straight, always leaving her house in the wee hours of the morning and going directly to Greenport. She was insatiable in and out of the bedroom, both sexually and intellectually. She had read everything I had read and more. As Joe I didn't think I should come across as particularly well-versed in literature, but I let her give me books and then we discussed them and her taste was impeccable. I'd already read most of what she gave me—Shelley, Woolf, Atwood, Robinson—but I pretended I didn't, and I read them for a second time just to have them fresh in my mind when we talked long into the nights. The lies came easier, which helped me relax and continue lying in a wicked circle, like a snake devouring its own tail.

If I arrived early enough I'd catch her painting, oftentimes in nothing but a long white T-shirt she could toss aside.

"I did my first painting the day of my mother's funeral," she revealed on one of those days, not speaking directly to me but to the canvas while I stood back and admired her.

The canvases still terrified me, her life-size emotions thrown against a glaring white background, but I'd grown to appreciate them as I appreciated her.

"I went to the funeral service. I had flown home alone, and I was alone that night in my childhood bed and I couldn't sleep. I ripped the sheet off the bed and found some shoe polish in the kitchen and I painted with that. And then . . . I never stopped."

"Your husband didn't go home with you to your mother's funeral?"

The only thing that made her clam up was the subject of Sam.

"Stop asking me about him, Joe. I really do not have much to say about him," she said. "We live entirely separate lives." She turned to me. "Why do you think you are here?"

But I didn't stop. I tried another night as we watched the sun set from her wraparound porch. We were sipping whiskey cocktails she'd made with herbs she told me she grew in the backyard, a jungle that resembled something out of Grey Gardens.

"How close is Sam to finishing the new novel? Have you read any of it?"

That time she slammed her drink down on the porch railing and walked inside. I knew I'd screwed up, and I took my time, at least five minutes before joining her. When I walked into the house I found her sitting quietly on the couch. "Take your pants off," she ordered me. "Take them off now." I began to unbutton my shirt.

"No, no. Just your pants. Underwear too."

With Elisabetta I always did what I was told.

"Now I want you to bend over the couch," she insisted. "Bend over the couch and do not look at me." She stood and pulled a purple scarf from her pocket. She tied it over my eyes, tight but not too tight, and I didn't ask her to adjust it. I heard her walk up the stairs and then back down. Before I knew what was happening I felt a sharp pain on my backside and then another. She was spanking me with something hard, wood, maybe. She did it again, and I couldn't help myself, I groaned with both pleasure and pain, feeling myself become hard against the couch. As much as it hurt, I also enjoyed it. I enjoyed it very much.

"Do you like this?" she asked, leaning into me, her breath wet in my ear. "Do you want more of it?"

"Yes," I said it quietly, almost a whisper.

"Well then I think I will take a little break." And she did. She left me like that, bent over the couch, panting and wanting more for ten minutes. She didn't tell me not to move, but I got the sense that's what she wanted and so I stayed there. When she returned she ran her fingernails down my back, hard enough to pierce the skin. They lingered on my backside, massaging the area where she had hit me. Now her hands were gentle, rubbing the skin, reaching between my legs to cradle my balls in her hand and then stroke me up and down. We stayed like that, with her leaning over me for a minute, and then she returned upright and proceeded to spank me again.

"Do you want me to do it harder?"

"Yes," I sputtered. I did and I didn't. The pain was unlike anything I had ever felt.

"Roll over," she instructed me. I did as I was told. With the blindfold in place I had no idea what was going to happen, and I found the uncertainty delicious. My life was so devoid of surprises, good or bad, that I couldn't help but find myself enjoying the mystery, practically begging for it, thirsty for even more.

She lowered herself slowly on top of me, and I groaned, hardly able to contain myself.

"Easy, boy," she said, continuing to raise and lower her hips in a rhythm that pleased her.

I thought about anything that would make me last longer—baseball statistics, game theory, Margaret Thatcher naked playing baseball and reciting game theory, but nothing worked, and the second Elisabetta threw her head back and screamed in satisfaction I let myself go.

Elisabetta fell asleep soon after. This had become a pattern of ours. She napped, and I read. Sometimes I'd cook us dinner, small uncomplicated dishes, pasta tossed with whatever happened to be in the fridge. But that night I found myself restless, and soon after she closed her eyes I began wandering around the house. It was always clean on Thursdays because Elisabetta had a service come in to scrub and sweep for hours before Hartwell came in for the weekend. Otherwise the house was a disaster. "I don't have anything against cleaning," she had said to me once. "It is not some kind of women's-lib thing. In fact, I find your American feminists terribly boring. I just also find cleaning very boring, and there are so many other things I would rather be doing with my time."

I needed to know more about the man who was with Elisabetta when I wasn't. I wanted Elisabetta, and I wanted to work with Sam, and the two things had become violently intertwined.

The house was a warren of interconnected rooms. I wandered up to the second floor and then the third. I knew I was snooping, invading their privacy. But I kept telling myself I was merely curious. Elisabetta had never told me not to roam. The house narrowed the higher I went, and the third floor had only two rooms, one a turret with an actual widow's walk where I imagined Victorian wives pacing as they waited for their husbands to return from sea. The other room was sparse, but it had equally stunning views of the ocean. There was a single desk and a high-backed leather chair facing the water.

On the desk was a typewriter covered by stacks and stacks of paper. Once again, I was rewarded for doing something I knew was wrong.

Sam Hartwell's manuscript. Or a copy of it, at least. There had to be at least one thousand pages, maybe more.

I couldn't help myself. I'd tried and tried to get Elisabetta to tell me any small nugget about what Hartwell was writing, and she refused. I started to think that perhaps even she didn't know. I listened at the stairs to make sure she hadn't woken up and took a stack of pages into the bathroom, figuring if she did wake up and find me in there I could make some kind of excuse and replace the pages later without her knowing. That's how I found myself lying prone in a claw-foot tub reading the beginning of Sam Hartwell's new novel.

First drafts are rarely masterpieces. The magic often happens when the right editor is paired with the right writer. But this book hardly needed anything. The words leaped off the page. I couldn't get through them fast enough. I wanted more, and before I knew it I had to get up and replace the pages with a new batch.

This much was clear: the book was about Elisabetta.

An angel-faced Italian peasant girl, just sixteen years old. I did the math. If these pages were truly autobiographical that meant Sam was in his thirties when she was just a teenager. The girl in the book came from a large conservative family, and the protagonist—it was written in the first person—was hitchhiking through the Italian countryside. The girl rejected him over and over again because he was American and he was old and she already had a successful career modeling in Paris, successful enough that she was supporting her mother and father and seven brothers and sisters. But the more she rejected him, the more he pursued her. He followed her from the village to Milan to Paris and New York and back again. He never gave up. The story also jumped around in time, going back in history to tell the love story between the girl's parents and then her grandparents before them, Russian nesting dolls of complicated courtship sagas. It wasn't just a captivating story. It was the way Hartwell told it. The writing was completely different from *Desolation Wilderness*, which was bold and brash and utterly masculine. This was sensitive and inquisitive, filled with the kind of humility that only a lifetime can give to a writer.

It was hours before I heard a thump downstairs and Elisabetta's voice calling up to me.

I slipped out of the bathroom and replaced the pages on the desk, hastily making sure I arranged them in their proper order. Then I returned to the bathroom and started running the water as I called down to her.

"I thought I'd take a bath," I said. "Would you like to join me?"

She appeared suddenly in the doorway, wearing nothing at all. "I thought you'd abandoned me."

"Never this early," I said, my head spinning with Hartwell's prose. I couldn't get enough of Elisabetta in the flesh nor on the page. The book was surely a masterpiece. I needed more, but I'd have to wait.

"I think a bath sounds like a lovely idea. I'll get some bubbles."
I wondered if she meant champagne or something for the tub.
Knowing her she would return with both. She turned and padded
back down the stairs, and I was finally able to breathe again. I
willed my heart to slow and stripped off my clothes, leaving them
in a puddle on the floor.

I didn't hear her come back upstairs, but suddenly she was
there. No bubble bath. No champagne. Instead, she had one of
her husband's suits slung over the crook of her elbow and two of
his ties in her other hand.

"I have a better idea. Put this on," she instructed me. I worried it wouldn't fit me. Sam had seemed much smaller than me
when I saw him onstage at the Whole Love benefit, but perhaps it
was an older suit, or maybe I wasn't as large as I thought I was. It
smelled faintly of tobacco and something spicy, and it was disconcerting to be wearing another man's clothes. Elisabetta demanded
that I lie facedown on the bed. I obeyed. She sat on my backside
and leaned forward to use the ties to bind my wrists to the head-
board, her hard nipples just grazing my upper back. I thought I
was ready for what was coming next, but the truth was I was never
ready for what she chose to do to me. She pulled the suit pants
down to my knees and began smacking me hard with her hand
on my left cheek. It was a different sensation when flesh struck
flesh. The knots on my wrists were so tight I could hardly move
my upper body, but I squirmed in discomfort anyway because I
knew that's what she wanted. White heat flashed in front of my
eyes from the sharp pain. I thought then about Hartwell wearing
this suit while he wrote, and I started to get hard. Maybe this was
the closest I would ever get to the great writer, wearing his clothes,
feeling his wife take out all her ire on my flesh. My entire body

shuddered when she stopped and reached her hand around to feel how hard I was. She squeezed me and bit the soft skin where my shoulder met my neck. I could feel how excited she was, but then she rolled off me, and before I knew what was happening she had turned off the light, left the room, and shut the door. She left me that way for hours, and I finally fell asleep. When I woke up, the ties were gone, I'd been stripped down to just my own underwear, and Elisabetta was curled on my chest. When she raised her head to look at me her eyes were wide and innocent. The morning sun brought out the gold flecks around her irises.

"Good morning, Elisabetta," I whispered dreamily.

"I think I'd like it if you called me Bette now," she mewed, and fell back to sleep.

CHAPTER NINE

"You need to pay up."

Kit's face was buried deep in her ledger, and I wanted to say something that would make her smile. I needed a distraction. I hadn't seen Elisabetta in nearly a week, not since the night I stole a look at the manuscript.

Since Sam's schedule was erratic, we'd developed this code of sorts. She would tie her scarf, the purple one, always the purple one, to the post on the widow's walk once he had left for the week. I could see the turret from my boat and I would know it was safe to return.

It hadn't been safe in six days.

I'd keep waiting, but until then, I'd have to stay busy, and the last thing I felt like doing was going back to meet up with Sperry and Posie for a garden-themed party at someone's Southampton share house. It was a garden-themed party, not a garden party. That meant the guests dressed as trees and gnomes and watering cans. Sperry had even purchased a leaf blower for it. The hosts thought the idea was terribly clever.

"What are you talking about?" Kit finally looked up. "Pay up?"

"The bet. On my first day you bet me I wouldn't last a week, and now I've lasted more than a month, so you need to pay up."

"What did we bet?"

"I don't think we discussed the terms."

"Well, what do you want?"

"A beer."

"Just one beer?"

"Maybe two. Maybe an order of fries."

"And when do you want this?"

"Tonight?"

She paused for a moment, and I was sure she was going to say no. "Why not."

"Feisty Crab?"

"Only if you want salmonella."

"Yikes."

"I'll take you somewhere good," Kit said. "I did lose the bet after all."

Kit threw a cardigan on over her T-shirt and looked ready to go. She drove a beat-up yellow Volkswagen Golf, and I agreed to go in her car with her. The radio was tuned to a classic rock station and the car was pristine except for a bunch of books in the back seat.

"I inherited her from my brothers. She was in a real bad state when they got ahold of her. They pretty much rebuilt the entire engine." Kit swept her hand around the car.

I knew nothing about engines, but this one grumbled and smoked a little like an angry dragon. It didn't sound like one that had recently been serviced. We drove out of Greenport and toward East Marion.

Kit tapped her fingers on the steering wheel to the opening

notes of "Under Pressure." She whispered the words softly . . .
"'Under pressure,'" as if no one else was sitting in the car with
her. Before I knew it she was belting out the lyrics.

"'It's the terror of knowing what the world is about . . .'"

She had a voice. It wasn't good, but it wasn't bad. I used to
wish I knew more about music, that I had more passion for particular artists. I always thought it would make me a more interesting person if I did.

I clapped when it was over, not even caring if it made me seem
like a dork.

"You like Bowie, huh?"

Without saying anything she flung her right foot up onto the
center console and, with one hand still on the wheel, pointed out
a thin black tattoo on her ankle. I'd noticed it, but never looked
very closely. Now I could see it was a Bowie knife stuck through
a small heart.

"He's completely real, man. My dad and my brothers never
understood. Always called him this fairy Brit. He wasn't their type
of musician. They liked their Springsteen and their Dylan. Did
you ever hear the story about Bowie and his long hair?"

"No," I replied.

"When he was just seventeen he got interviewed by the BBC
as the founder of a group called the Society for the Prevention of
Cruelty to Long-Haired Men. He actually said, 'You know it's not
nice when people call you darling.'"

"Was he being serious or messing with them?"

Kit slammed the heel of her hand on the steering wheel.
"That's just it. Who knows? He didn't give a damn what anyone
thought about him, and that's what I love about him."

Before I could respond, Kit took an exit I'd never taken and pulled into the parking lot of an unassuming cottage right on the water.

"This is where all the fishermen come to eat good fish," she said as she slammed the door. "And a lot of those fancy chefs from over on the other side of the bay come here too. Martha makes the best fish and chips you'll ever have in your entire life."

"I get a fish dinner too? I thought you said it was just fries and a beer."

Kit smiled. "When I lose a bet I always pay up right."

Martha's had none of the kitsch of the Feisty Crab. It was a simple room with plain wooden tables and benches. Nothing hung on the walls. After ordering a couple bottles of beer, we headed out to a deck outside that cozied up to the shore.

A waitress appeared to take our orders. "I don't think we've seen a menu yet," I said.

Kit laughed. "There isn't one. Martha makes what Martha wants. You get the fish that's been caught today."

"What's been caught today?" I asked the waitress, who seemed to enjoy Kit's schooling me in the ways of Martha's.

"We have a ton of scallops."

I looked to Kit for approval.

"Scallops, whatever you're frying up, and some chips."

"How do you know Martha?"

"Everyone knows Martha."

"I don't know Martha."

"You're new." Kit smirked at me.

"Can I meet her?"

"Maybe."

I had been pulling crabs, scallops, stripers, and fluke out of the water every day. You'd think I'd never want to see another fish again, much less eat one, but I'd developed a newfound respect for everything it took to get the fish from the sea onto the plate. I finished my beer quickly and put my hand up for another.

"That was fast."

"I was thirsty," I defended myself.

"So, pretty boy? How are you liking the job?"

"I love it."

"Really?"

"Yeah." I thought about how I wanted to explain it to her. "It feels really good. Going out there on the water with nothing and coming back with something." Geez. That sounded stupid and simple. "It's hard," I tried. "It's really hard work. But after a long day out there you feel like you accomplished something."

She peeled at the label of the beer bottle with her chewed-down fingernails.

"Yeah. My dad used to say something like that. He liked the fact that he was going out and getting something people really needed to survive. He used to say it was a hell of a lot more fulfilling than tinkering with people's Lamborghinis. He was a mechanic before he was a fisherman."

"Your dad has taught me a lot," I said. "Not just about fishing. He's been good to me. Patient."

I didn't want to go on and on, but getting to work with Eddie was the best part of the job, listening to his tall tales, to him belting out Billy Joel, feeling like I was his friend and equal. That all meant a lot to me.

"What about you?" What *about* Kit? She was a complete mystery. She'd grown up around those boats with her father. Eddie had told me that much. The men who worked them practically raised her after her mother, Brenda, picked up and left a little over a decade ago.

"What about me?" She was being coy now. The label came loose from the beer bottle and fluttered onto the floor and out over the deck.

The scallops arrived before she had to answer, lightly seared and drizzled with lemon. They were delicious, tender, but not chewy. They tasted like they'd just come out of the ocean. I couldn't help but let my mind wander to the first night I spent with Elisabetta, where she described soaking her scallops in butter and them melting in her mouth. Even the tiniest glimmer of her got me excited, and I needed to put a stop to it so I could pay attention to Kit. I wasn't messing around or anything. I actually wanted to get to know her better.

"Seriously though. Tell me about you," I said, burying Elisabetta in my thoughts. "What do you want to do with the rest of your life?

Kit made a noise between a laugh and a grunt. It wasn't a friendly sound. "That's such a ridiculous question. What do you *want* to do? Who really gets to do what they want to do? I feel like we're setting kids up to be unhappy when we ask them that right at the start of kindergarten. You get a group of bright-eyed little five-year-olds saying they want to be astronauts and game-show hosts and athletes and scientists, and how many of those things actually happen?"

I had asked the question because it felt like the right question to ask to start a conversation. But maybe I'd also asked it because I wanted to hear someone else's answer. Since before I could remember I'd been told I would follow in my father's footsteps. I'd never had a choice in the matter. And because I'd never had a choice I always said I wanted to be a book publisher. It didn't matter if it was true.

"For now I need to do this," Kit continued. "Because if I don't do it, then no one else will. Dad can't keep his own books. We'd go bankrupt because he'd say yes every time someone asked him for a loan. He needs me. And as long as he needs me I'm not going anywhere."

"But what if you could do anything?" Once the words were out of my mouth I realized that she had already made it very clear that she didn't want to answer this kind of question, and I wished I could take it back. I wanted us to have a fun night together.

I heard the loud bang of a door slamming shut. A portly woman with a shock of gray curly hair emerged from the kitchen and rushed over to us. She wrapped her arms around Kit's shoulders and kissed her on the forehead.

"My baby girl," she clucked as she smushed Kit's face against her.

Kit managed to turn her face away from the massive bosom. "Joe. You wanted to meet Martha. Here is Martha."

"Are you on a date, Kitty Kat?"

"Jesus. Awkward much." Kit blushed. I had never seen her blush before. It started at her jawline and moved slowly across her face. "No. He works with Daddy."

"A fisherman!" Martha raised two bushy eyebrows in surprise.

"For the summer," Kit said. "And then I think he might be onto bigger and better things."

It wasn't the first time I had wondered whether Kit fully bought into my story. There was something in the tone of her voice that made me think she didn't.

"I need to come over and see your dad. Cook a meal for him. How's he hanging in there?"

"Oh, you know. The same," Kit said.

"I'll come by on Sunday night."

"That'll be nice."

The blush still colored Kit's face when Martha returned to the kitchen.

"I know this isn't a date," I said to reassure her.

"She's just a busybody. Always telling me it's time I get out there and find a man. Like I don't have better things to do. Like finding a man solves any more problems than it causes. And besides, she doesn't practice what she's preaching."

She leaned in closer to me and told me about how Martha and Eddie had grown up together. "Right next door. They were close as brother and sister until they were eighteen, and then my dad started dating my mom and Mom didn't like Martha that much. I think maybe Martha loved my dad a little, but she'd always been too afraid to tell him. It was hard on her. They became friends again after my mom left, but it was never entirely the same."

"She sounded worried about your dad."

"Everyone is worried about my dad. I'm worried about my dad."

"Why?"

"The commercial fishing companies are putting the little guys like us out of business faster than you can say Long John Silver. We're small potatoes and meanwhile the cost of doing business is through the roof. It's hard as hell to find reliable employees. They're constantly turning over." She pushed some fries around her plate. "I don't know how much longer we can keep going. Plus, his health is total shit. He smokes two packs of cigarettes a day and has a fifth of whiskey before he goes to bed."

I'd known that Eddie's business wasn't exactly raking it in, but I didn't realize things were as bad as Kit was saying. He seemed to take it all in stride. Some of his calmness had even worn off on me.

"What happens if you can't keep the business going?"

Kit sighed. "It could be for the best. Who knows. Dad could sell the house. There might be money in it. He could go live with my brother Larry in Jersey. He's right in Hoboken. They've got room and two kids and they're dying to have him there. But he's proud. I don't think that would ever happen, and I can't leave him."

The waitress came and took our plates. A minute later she returned with a berry cobbler heaped with vanilla bean ice cream.

"Compliments of Martha." She smiled as she placed it in front of Kit. "She says she heard the news and she's real proud of you."

The blush returned, stronger this time. With color in her cheeks Kit softened and looked younger, sweeter.

"What's she proud of?" I asked once the waitress was gone. I knew that I was being nosy.

"Dammit. I wonder who told her."

"Who told her what?"

"I got into this school. This program for hotel administration. I just found out that I got off the wait list, but I don't know . . ." She trailed off.

"That's great!" I hadn't even realized that was something she was interested in. "Congratulations! What school?"

Her face flushed with either pride or humility. "Cornell."

The name of the Ivy League school caught me off guard, and I immediately felt like an asshole for it. Kit was smart as hell. Why should I be surprised that she got in somewhere like that, somewhere that had happened to reject me, even?

"It doesn't matter," she continued, an edge of bitterness seeping into her voice. "We can't pay for it. I applied for a couple of scholarships and never heard anything back. And besides, Dad needs me." She scooped a heaping spoonful of ice cream into her mouth. A little smudge of vanilla remained on the side of her lips.

"So now you know what I want to be when I grow up," Kit said once she'd swallowed.

"You want to work in a hotel?"

"I want to *run* my own hotel," she corrected me, the bitterness replaced with a shy grin. "There's this old place out at Sparkling Pointe. It's a dump right now, but it's got a little vineyard and it's like ten rooms and there are some cottages on the property. I have these fantasies of buying it and fixing it up myself and turning it into a bed-and-breakfast and little winery. Who knows . . . maybe the North Fork could be as fancy as the South one day."

I liked her like this, dreamy and filled with lofty expectations. She dug her spoon into the cobbler and released a long sigh of pleasure after putting it in her mouth.

"You need to try this," she said.

I didn't think I could possibly eat another bite of anything—we'd had so much fish and chips and scallops—but I couldn't deny her.

"This is the best thing I've ever put in my mouth," I agreed with her after swallowing the delicious cobbler.

"I know, right? First thing I would do at my B and B is hire Martha to do all the food." She chewed, considering. "It's a stupid dream."

"It's not," I insisted.

"It is. And it will never happen." Kit took the last bite and asked the waitress for the check.

She just waved her away. "You're not paying. Get out of here."

Kit dug around in her purse and left a twenty for a tip on the table.

"You sure know how to pay out a bet, Delgado," I said as we walked off the deck and down onto the beach. Kit wandered down the sand to the edge of the water and kicked off her shoes, letting the waves wash over her toes.

I nudged at the surrendered shell of a horseshoe crab with the tip of my toe.

"In kindergarten, when all the teachers asked you what you wanted to be when you grew up what did you tell them?" I asked her. "Hotel owner?"

"Firefighter," Kit responded almost immediately. I could see a faint flicker of a smile play at her lips. "My uncle Rick was one down in Riverhead, and I thought it was the best job ever because he let me ride in the back of this big red truck and wear his helmet."

"Jobs with mandatory hats are indeed dreamy."

She punched me in the arm in an adorable way.

"How about you?"

I couldn't tell her the truth, but I could tell her something that was true.

"I'd like to write a book. A really good book, not some throwaway beach read, but something that sticks with people. Something they remember."

"Oh," she said with a small flicker of surprise.

It was true. If I were honest with myself it was the reason I had such mixed feelings about going into business with my father. I wanted to be the one creating the characters and stories rather than the one who shepherded them into the world.

"But it will probably never happen," I said with certainty. I'd never admitted wanting to be a writer out loud to anyone because it sounded like such a terrible cliché.

"I get it. That's the thing about dreams. They're all just clichés. I shouldn't have told you mine. My stupid dreams," she said.

"I'm glad you did. I'd like to see the property sometime."

"It's at the end of Kenneys Road. You can't miss it. Drive out there if you want."

"I'd like to go with you," I said, and meant it. Everything about the night had felt good and comfortable. It was the opposite of how I felt like when I was with Elisabetta, like every breath might be my last and I wouldn't care.

Kit turned and tilted her head to look up to me. Her fierce little chin wobbled slightly. For a moment I wondered what would happen if I leaned down and kissed her. Would she kiss me back? I imagined that for all her bravado, Kit would be more timid than Elisabetta.

As quickly as she'd looked up at me, she turned away and began walking back to the car. "Come on, pretty boy. I should get you back to the dock before you turn into a pumpkin."

CHAPTER TEN

The last thing I wanted was a roommate, but I didn't really have a choice.

Sperry's dad and Kelli-Anne were splitting up. Maybe just for the summer, but also maybe for good. It was difficult to get the entire story about what happened, but it either had to do with Sperry's dad sleeping with one of their Central American cleaning women or the fact that he refused to let Kelli-Anne adopt a seventh Chihuahua. Both of those things were true, but who knows which was the straw that broke the camel's back. If I had to wager I would guess it was the Chihuahua.

In their haste to come to a separation agreement, Kelli-Anne was retaining ownership of the house for the rest of the summer.

"She won't ever get it for good," Sperry insisted. "My father is the MacGyver of prenups. But she does have it through Labor Day, which means—"

Oh no.

"I have to move in with you."

I didn't want Sperry living with me for a number of reasons, chief among them the fact that he would realize I was hardly ever home during the week and would start asking questions I didn't want to answer. But I'd never been able to say no to him, and I didn't have a good enough reason to start now, so I agreed to help him move in on a Tuesday afternoon.

I hated the fact that I needed to skip work and another chance to possibly see Elisabetta. The scarf still wasn't tied to the post on the turret. That fact worried me when I allowed it to. What if she'd discovered my snooping? What if she never wanted to see me again?

Sperry had an awful lot of stuff for a twenty-two-year-old man. The boat shoes alone took a single trip between the two houses. He also had all these bow ties and summer suits and, of course, there was Mrs. Frankweiler, Sperry's obese one-eyed tabby cat. Sperry had found the cat about fifteen years ago as a one-eyed kitten shivering in a rainstorm beneath one of his father's classic cars. Sperry heard the kitten's mewling and crawled on his belly beneath the car. She was no bigger than his hand, but she fought him with everything she had as he pulled her out and brought her into the house. We'd just read that wonderful book about a brother and a sister who ran away from their fancy Connecticut families to take up residence in the Metropolitan Museum of Art, and, like every fancy kid raised within a thirty-mile radius of Central Park, we maintained our own fantasies of running away and sleeping in the Temple of Dendur.

"This cat is an old soul," eight-year-old Sperry determined to me. "She's Mrs. Frankweiler." It was a strange thing to call a tiny adorable kitten, but Mrs. Frankweiler grew into her name in no time. Since that fateful night under the car Mrs. Frankweiler lived in the lap of luxury, traveling everywhere Sperry went, including Dartmouth, where he got an apartment in Hanover because pets weren't allowed in the dorms. With his revolving door of stepmothers and au pairs (including the au pair who became a stepmother), Mrs. Frankweiler was the one constant in Sperry's life.

"You need to find me a discreet cleaner at the end of the summer," I reminded him as he carried the cat over his shoulder to my house. "A good one. Deidre's allergic."

He guffawed. "That's just a lie she told you because she didn't want to get you a dog." He placed the cat on the ground, and she trotted happily next to him the rest of the way.

"I appreciate this, man," he said when it was through, and slapped me on the back when it was through. "Let me take you to dinner." I agreed as long as we could go somewhere low-key and as long as it could be just the two of us. I didn't feel like spending the evening listening to Posie describe her business plan for an Internet company that would let you bid on other people's vintage clothes from the privacy of your own home.

"Let's just go to Wolfie's." I said it like I didn't really want to go, but I actually loved Wolfie's, the one-time haunt of Jackson Pollock and Willem de Kooning. Wolfie's was the perfect dive bar in one of the last middle-class neighborhoods in the Hamptons. It was still a place where the locals went for beers, and because of that they hadn't raised their prices in years, which meant the owners were constantly worrying about how to make the rent. The paint on the yellow walls was peeling, the barstools constantly wobbled, and the pool table was scuffed to hell, but Wolfie's was a place you could go alone and sit at the bar and have a beer and a real conversation with a stranger. No one was looking over his or her shoulder to see who might come through the door next.

Sperry was wearing these salmon-colored shorts with little anchors embroidered on them, and I thought maybe he should change before we went to Wolfies, but I didn't know exactly how to mention it, so I let it slide.

"Do you think Kelli-Anne and your dad will actually get a divorce?" I asked him once we settled in at a table in the corner. It was still early, not even five, and we were among just a few early patrons in the place. The four other guys sitting at the bar looked like they had just gotten off a construction job. Their boots were muddy, their brows greasy with the sweat of a long day's work.

"Who knows. My dad has made a real art out of marrying poorly," Sperry said. "But he seems to be having fun, and he can afford it. This is annoying, but hey, at least it means we get to spend some more time together. I feel like I haven't seen you all summer."

I nodded slowly as I took a sip of my beer.

"How's Posie?" I asked.

"We're not a thing anymore."

"I didn't know."

"You've been MIA, dude."

"Well, what happened?"

"She decided to try being a lesbian for a little bit."

"For a little bit?"

"Or forever. She took one of her dad's cars and drove across the country with Sierra. I think they're somewhere in the Rockies by now, though Sierra's got some friends who own a pot farm in the Santa Cruz mountains, so maybe they'll end up there."

"So Sierra is gay?"

Sperry shrugged. "I guess. I didn't ask many questions."

"I'm sorry, man."

"Hey, love is love." He finished his drink. "It was for the best. I hated wearing those thongs. What about you? Any decent action this summer?"

Decent action. Those weren't the right words to describe what had happened to me for the past month. In fact, I couldn't find the right words, so I shook my head and pretended there was no action at all.

"I could hook you up with Beth."

"She's like your sister."

"But she's so hot."

"It's still gross."

We made our way through a couple of burgers and some fries. I knew I was going to have to give Sperry some kind of explanation if he was going to be living in my house.

"I kind of took this job," I mumbled.

He raised his eyebrows. "Oh yeah? A summer thing?"

I quickly ran through ways I could explain it to him in my head. In the end I went for the simplest answer.

"I'm working on a fishing boat across the bay. In Greenport." Telling the truth was something of a relief.

"You're fishing?" Sperry didn't get it at first. "On your boat?"

"No. For a fishing company. I fish on someone else's boat."

"And you sell the fish?"

"I do. Well, they do. I just catch the fish."

He considered it for a moment.

"Well, that is fucking fantastic," he said suddenly, and slammed his hand down on the table so hard it rattled.

"Yeah," I said. "Yeah, it is."

"And all this time I thought you were avoiding me."

"Come on, man."

"I'll bet the chicks love it. You coming in on the boat and all."

I thought about Kit then. She didn't love it. I didn't think she thought much of the fact that I worked on a boat at all. Now that I knew she'd gotten into Cornell, there was a part of me that thought maybe she would accept the real Henry Cane, maybe even like him.

"They think I'm kind of a pansy."

Sperry chuckled at that. "Because you are kind of a pansy. But you are a very special kind of pansy, dildo. A very special pansy indeed."

It was Kit who met me on the boat the next day. Her short hair was scraped back into a jaunty little ponytail and she wore knee-high rubber wellie boots.

"I'm going out with you today."

"You?"

"Me. Dad's laid up with the flu, maybe it's a hangover, I don't know. We've got more orders than we can fill if we take one boat out of commission, so it's you and me."

"Let's get on the water, matey."

"I don't do the eel hooking," she said, looking over her shoulder. "I was embarrassed to tell you that, but I'm telling you straightaway. I can't put the hook in their little eyes. I just can't. So don't ask, and we'll be fine."

Kit was the last person I expected to be squeamish about bait. It was cute. "I can do the eels." The amazing thing was that was finally true. I'd gotten perfectly capable of doing everything that needed doing on the boat, and even though I would miss Eddie, there was a part of me that was excited to captain the boat on my own.

Kit had the agility and speed of someone who had been working boats her entire life. By noon we already had a good haul, but we stayed out. Eddie and I often went back to our tried-and-true spots, but Kit pushed me out of Plum Gut and around the tip of Plum Island, moving us out toward Connecticut.

"Get out of your comfort zone, pretty boy."

We spent the next hour talking about life and music. She knew a lot more than I did about the kinds of cool indie bands that I always wished I knew more about. She told me about her brothers, the bouncer and the hairdresser. "I let him give me a body wave when I was younger, and he made me look like Albert Einstein crossed with early Jon Bon Jovi," she laughed. She was more at ease on the water than she was behind the desk, and I wished there was a way to release her from the burden of her ledgers and books, but I didn't dare bring it up again.

"What about your dad? What's he like when he isn't at work?"

"The same," she said. A cold look passed over her face. "I wish he'd meet someone, though. I honestly don't think he's been with anyone since my mother. They'd been together since they were sixteen. Isn't that insane?"

I considered Elisabetta and Sam for a moment. She met him when she was a teenager. "Yeah. He must have loved her an awful lot."

"Too much," Kit corrected me. "He loved her too much, and it almost ruined his life." She paused. "I look exactly like her. It's weird. The older I get, the more I look like her. I catch him staring at me every so often, and I know he sees her face, and I feel guilty for looking like her."

"Do you ever hear from her?"

"She sends Christmas cards. She lives out in Idaho on some hippie commune where they grow all their own food and raise each other's children, which is ironic, because she couldn't finish raising her own." Kit's face contorted into a look of disgust, but then one of the rods rattled and she quickly moved to reel it in.

She unhooked a flounder and threw it in the bucket.

"So," she said, wiping her hands. "What would you write if you wrote a book?"

I had notebooks filled with ideas that never panned out, but none of those came to mind. Instead, I thought about Hartwell's novel, the pages stacked neatly on the desk on the third floor of the old house.

"It all starts when this American guy decides to go hitchhiking around the Italian countryside."

Kit rolled her eyes at that.

"Come on . . . it gets better."

It wasn't the book I would write. It was the book I desperately wanted to edit. Maybe the only book I wanted to edit. As I recounted the plot to Kit I thought of all the notes and suggestions I would make as an editor and publisher if only I could wrest it away from Sam. I'd spent a good portion of the past few weeks thinking of ways I might ask Elisabetta to help me convince her husband to publish his book with Empirical. All of them required me telling her that I had lied to her, which would almost certainly involve her expelling me from her house and never speaking to me again.

Kit listened to Hartwell's story, every so often pulling in a fishing line. I stopped abruptly, right at the spot where I had stopped reading the manuscript.

"Keep going," she said. "How does it end?"

"I don't know," I told her truthfully.

"It's a nice story."

A nice story? It was a wonderful story, a sweeping and epic tale of love across generations and continents.

She continued. "It feels a little self-indulgent, on the part of the male protagonist. Like, he just expects this woman will fall in love with him and he can't imagine why she wouldn't? He pursues her until she has no choice but to give in."

To be honest I hadn't thought about it like that. To me the protagonist's persistence was romantic. To Kit it was an act of attrition. I supposed in reality it had been somewhere in the middle.

We took the long way home, gliding around the east side of Shelter Island because Kit wanted me to.

"I used to see dolphins out here sometimes when I was a kid . . . right past Ram Island," she shouted, her hair whipping in the wind, forming a halo around her head.

I wanted to indulge her rare whimsy. I hoped a part of her was enjoying my company as much as I enjoyed hers.

"Here. Stop right here," she said, and pointed at a spot with no discernible significance.

We cracked open a couple of beers and lingered at the mouth of the Peconic.

"Who took you to see the dolphins?" I asked her.

"Eddie," she said, her eyes fixed on the water, her beer nearly untouched. She was quiet for a minute at least. "And my mother. My mother came with us a couple of times."

"Do you miss her?" I asked carefully.

Kit never took her eyes off the waves. "Sometimes I think I miss the idea of her. How can you miss someone you never really knew?"

There it was. A silvery flash above the water. If I didn't know exactly what we were looking for I would have missed it.

"There they are!" Kit's melancholy over my previous question evaporated like a puff of smoke as she squealed like a little girl. For a moment I marveled at how I found her lovelier the more time we spent together, with each little chink of her armor that she let fall away.

"Just one?" I said with mock disappointment. The truth was the sight of a dolphin made me giddy inside. For as long as I'd been taking my own boat out in these waters, I had yet to spy a dolphin.

"If there's one on the surface, there are a dozen down below," Kit said with an adorable grin. She stripped off her tank top and stepped out of her shorts. She stood there on the deck for a moment in just her tattered white bra and saggy underwear before she dove off the boat.

"You'll scare them away," I called out to her.

"They're not going to be scared by little old me. Are you coming?"

I only hesitated because the boat wasn't properly anchored, but the wind was light and the current weak, and I promised myself I wouldn't swim out too far. Kit dove beneath the surface, and when she reappeared there were two more dolphins leaping in front of her.

"They like to play," she shouted.

I gingerly unbuttoned my shirt and dropped my shorts, grateful I had thought to put on clean underwear that morning.

The Atlantic Ocean is always colder than you expect it to be and I got the initial shock when my body hit the water. I forced my eyes to open and adjust to the salt water. It was murky. The water flowing in from the sound always is, but I could see what looked like twelve or maybe more slender bodies wiggling below the surface.

"There's a whole bunch of them down there," I said when I came up for air.

"I told you," Kit said. Her white bra was now entirely see-through in the water, and I felt bad looking. She dove below again, and I followed her this time, pulling as much air as possible into my lungs, so I could dive even farther. The dolphins weren't just undisturbed by our presence. They actually seemed to enjoy it. They kept a cautious distance but always came back, leaping and splashing into the air. We kept diving and bobbing for nearly a half hour, before I realized we'd gotten awfully far away from the boat and the sun was falling dangerously close to the horizon.

"Hey, Kit. I've gotta get you home."

"Just five more minutes," she yelled, and dove beneath the surface.

I swam after her and playfully gripped her ankle. She spit a stream of water in my face when we came up for air, and before I could wipe my eyes she was back under.

"Have it your way." I paddled back to the boat and pretended I was about to leave her.

"I'll be fine out here with my friends," she yelled up at me.

"Will you?"

"Yes." She started to swim toward me. "But I'm starting to get hungry, so I guess I'll let you drag me away."

"Come on, Flipper." I reached a hand down to pull her out of the water.

I guided us down and around Mashomack and then West

Neck. There was just enough light left for me to look up at the turret as we rounded the bottom of Shelter Island. I saw it. The scarf waved in the wind like a welcoming flag. She wanted me tonight.

Kit had been drying off. She found an old fisherman's sweater down below and put it on instead of her wet clothes. It reached nearly to her knees, and she looked like a child as she walked over to me and wrapped her arms around my neck, burying her face in my chest.

"Thank you," she murmured. "Thank you for giving me such a perfect day."

"You're welcome." I stared over her head at the looming Victorian house and thought about how I'd never seen her smile as much as she had in the past couple of hours. A part of me wanted to keep making her smile.

"Want to go to Martha's?" she asked when she pulled away.

I wished that I could say yes, but I had no choice. I was a man obsessed.

"I can't tonight. I really need to get home. Rain check?" I asked it like I was asking for mercy.

The disappointment in her eyes stabbed me a little, but I leaned in and kissed her on the cheek anyway. It took another few minutes to ease the boat into the dock and tie her up.

"I'll hose her down," Kit said. "Get out of here." She stood on the deck as I climbed into my own boat. She lifted her hand in an anemic wave, and I turned to go.

CHAPTER ELEVEN

Elisabetta greeted me at the door completely nude.

"What if it wasn't me?" I said hello by kissing her hard on the mouth.

"Then someone else would have gotten quite a thrill." She laughed, her mouth open so wide I could see the pink of her tonsils. "Maybe I would have had to screw him too. Or her. Who knows?"

She was ready for me, practically ripping my still damp shirt from my body, loosening several buttons in the process. Before I knew what was happening, I was flat on my back in the foyer with the door wide open.

"Close it," I murmured into her neck as she straddled me.

"Leave it open. Let them watch." Not that there was anyone within watching distance, but I worried I wouldn't be able to perform with the door open to the world. She could have cared less.

I shouldn't have been concerned. I'd been imagining this for a week. I could have done it with the entire Empirical board of trustees watching.

I gave her exactly what she wanted.

I grasped her ass with both of my hands and pulled her into

me. She gasped as I sat up and then rose to my feet, keeping her legs wrapped around my waist the entire time. When we were upright I pressed her back against the hallway wall and plunged myself even deeper into her.

"I like you like this," she whispered, her words catching in her throat as I bit down on her earlobe.

When she came she screamed so loudly I worried it would wake folks across the sound. We collapsed into a heap, her heart pounding in unison with mine.

I wanted her again.

I also wanted the manuscript.

I hoped she'd take her regular nap, but instead she wanted to drink and chat and catch up. Once we'd recovered she poured both of us a glass of whiskey neat.

"I've missed you," she said after taking a long sip. "Sam stayed out here too long. He's almost finished writing, or so he says, and he wanted to celebrate. He invited all sorts of people to the house . . . society types. The opposite of you."

She said society types as though she were saying heroin addicts or pedophiles.

I wanted to tell her I missed her too. It was the truth, after all. But telling her I'd missed her didn't cover it. I'd longed for her. My yearning was a desperate thing, almost feral, and the power she had over me terrified me. So I didn't acknowledge it. I didn't say anything at all.

Maybe she didn't care if I responded. She kept talking. "This terrible woman was here. Sarah Knowles. She wants to do a profile of Sam and me for some Hamptons rag," she went on. "She was here with her husband, a scrawny little man, no bigger than my thumb. I was sick of hearing her talk, so I imagined them having sex instead . . . a teeny tiny little monkey riding a giraffe is what it would look like. When he comes he probably squeaks."

I had never once pictured Sarah Knowles and her husband, Bob Knowles, the petite executive producer of a morning television show, doing anything but playing tennis with my parents.

"Then this Sarah returned the next morning and asked me all kinds of ridiculous questions about me being Sam's muse, which is absurd, because he's never written a single word about me in his life and I wouldn't want him to."

Elisabetta hadn't read Sam's new manuscript. She had no idea.

We finished the whiskey. She asked if I wanted another, and I said yes because it was clear she did.

"Let me get some ice this time," I said gently, and took the glasses to the freezer. I returned with a pint of vanilla ice cream I'd found in the freezer and offered her a heaping spoonful. She smiled and let me feed her.

When the pint was nearly finished she took the spoon from me and scooped out the remaining ice cream. I opened my mouth wide like a baby bird, expecting her to return the favor. Instead, she raised the spoon above her head and hurled the ice cream at one of her grand canvases across the room. This one seemed more finished than the others, less sexual in nature, but still abstract. When I squinted I could make out the distinct outlines of mountains and trees and maybe the silhouette of a woman in the distance.

"He told me he hated it." She nodded at the painting.

"Who?" I asked, even though I didn't need to.

"I could suffocate him with his own pillow," Elisabetta said, staring at me and daring me to say something, anything. I didn't realize she'd been drinking before I got there. Clearly a lot. At least, enough.

"Who?" I asked again dumbly.

"He is a very sound sleeper, and he probably wouldn't even notice until it was too late. Or arsenic in his whiskey," she said. "Just a little sprinkle here and a sprinkle there. The doctors say that his heart is weak. It wouldn't take much."

I stroked her upper thigh in a way I knew that she liked and then moved my hand down between her legs. She was ready for me again. I rolled heavily on top of her, just to end the conversation about murdering her husband. She reached her hands onto my shoulders and then wrapped her slender fingers around my neck, squeezing once gently and then harder. I kept going, thrusting into her as she dug her nails into the soft skin on the back of my neck. We came together, and I knew that she would fall asleep after that. She rolled over onto her side and placed her head on a pillow that had already been tossed onto the floor.

"Oh, Joe. Will you be here when I wake up?"

"I will," I promised her. I poured myself another glass of wine and waited until her breathing slowed before I quietly made my way up the stairs to the second floor and then to the third.

The door to the office was locked. I jiggled the handle, convinced it was merely stuck. But after a full minute it looked like I was just frantically shaking hands with the door. I slumped onto the floor with my back to the door. The loss was even deeper than not seeing Elisabetta's scarf tied to that tower for days. I considered kicking the door in. It was an old house, with old locks. It couldn't be that hard to break it. What was I thinking? I'd never broken into anything in my life. I wasn't the kind of person who kicked down doors. Of course, a couple of months ago I wasn't the kind of person who slept with another man's wife.

I examined the thing. It was one of those antique locks, the kind that took a proper key, not the flimsy little things you buy in the hardware store but a well-crafted piece of metal. It had to be here somewhere.

I walked down one flight of stairs and into their bedroom. We rarely spent any time in there. If we came upstairs at all Elisabetta preferred to be in the guest room. I preferred it too. It let me keep Sam Hartwell out of my mind when I needed to.

I flicked on the light switch, and I took in the entire master bedroom. The room was neater than the downstairs, the bed actually made, clothes put away in their proper places. A window was open, and a cool breeze caused the curtains to flutter as if small children might be hiding behind them. I paused, caught off guard for a moment by my own reflection in the mirror above the dresser. A stranger stared back at me, one with a full beard, tanned skin the color of roasted chestnuts, and sun wrinkles cut into tributaries around the eyes. There was a new confidence to my posture. My entire body felt stronger from working the boats all day. I looked down at my hands and noticed half a thumbnail was missing and the skin beneath had turned a permanent violet and black.

At the start of the summer I had been a newly graduated, vaguely handsome young man partial to once-monthly haircuts and careful shaves. I hardly recognized this Neanderthal staring back at me, but I liked him.

A single silver picture frame sat on the imposing old oak dresser. I picked it up and studied it. The photo was black-and-white. The man in the photo looked like the Sam Hartwell of his author photo in *Desolation Wilderness*, an untamed younger man. The woman was young, but she was most definitely Elisabetta. In the photo her hair was chopped into a pixie cut that was quite becoming with her long face and sculpted cheekbones. She clutched Hartwell around the waist and gazed up at him with unconcealed adoration as he stared into the camera. It puzzled me that she would keep this photograph in her bedroom even though she professed to despise her husband as vehemently as she did. The photo had to be at least twenty-five years old, maybe older, and it was clear that she loved him then.

What had happened to the two of them in the past two decades? What had he done to make her despise him? It had to be in his novel. I had to get my hands on it.

Where would she put a key? I opened the top drawers of the dresser and found nothing but tangled piles of bras and panties on one side and neatly rolled white socks and Jockey underwear on the other. Maybe the nightstand. I rustled through the drawers on both sides, but both were empty, save for a King James Bible, which surprised me, until I realized it must have just come with the house.

I sat on the bed, defeated. I was ready to head back downstairs, maybe even break my promise to Elisabetta that I would be there when she woke up and just get on *Arabella* and go home. How could I hide my disappointment from her when she woke up? My anticipation for the manuscript had been so high that all my muscles ached with defeat. As I was about to turn off the light I spotted a small jewelry box tucked on a shelf amid stacks of hardcover books. It had the texture of the inside of a clamshell, a shiny pinkish pearl. My heart pounded as I opened the small box. The click of the hinges was louder than I expected, and I paused, convinced that it would wake Elisabetta.

It didn't, and I was rewarded with a box containing nothing but a single skeleton key. I was hasty but not stupid. I went back downstairs and checked that Elisabetta was still fast asleep. I even covered her with a blanket before taking the stairs back up two at a time.

I pulled the key from my pocket and slid it into the old brass lock. At first nothing happened. I wiggled it left, then right. I decided then and there, before I'd even managed to get the door open, that I would finish the manuscript that night. I couldn't wait any longer. If Elisabetta woke I would find a way to smuggle it out of the house and replace it before Hartwell returned from the city. Like Elisabetta, it had gotten ahold of me in such a primal way that not finishing it was no longer an option.

I entered the room and flicked on the light.

The desk was bare. The manuscript was gone.

CHAPTER TWELVE

Kit wasn't at the boat the next morning. I walked over to the office, and she wasn't there either. The place was a mess, like it had been robbed or something. An open window had allowed the morning wind to knock the ledger and all of the papers off the desk. They fluttered on the floor like defeated paper airplanes.

A red light on the answering machine blinked. I crossed the room and hit play to find a half-dozen messages from fishermen looking for either Eddie or Kit. I knew in my bones that something was very, very wrong.

When the phone rang I jumped, feeling like it had caught me doing something I wasn't supposed to be doing even though I'd just been standing in the middle of the room like an idiot.

I let it ring, and the person calling didn't leave a message. But when it rang a second time I felt obligated to pick it up.

"Hello?" I began tentatively.

"Who is this?"

"It's Henry."

"Who?"

"It's Joe."

"Joe?"

"Kit?"

She sighed into the phone. "Hey."

"Where are you? Are you okay?"

"We're at the hospital. Dad had a heart attack last night. I called because I thought one of the boys might be there, that someone could maybe let everyone know."

"Kit. I'm really sorry. Shit. Well, I'm here. What can I do?"

She told me where I could find a list of phone numbers for everyone who worked for Eddie and then a second list of numbers for all the restaurants and wholesalers he supplied. "Tell everyone we won't be doing any business today or tomorrow, but that we should come up with a plan by the end of the week. Tell everyone I'll be in touch then." She spoke quickly and efficiently, and I could hardly keep up.

"How is he? How are you?"

Her voice wobbled. "He's been better. I'm dealing." I thought about how happy she'd looked yesterday when we were on the boat, how she leaped into the sea to chase a pod of dolphins. I thought about how quickly that kind of happiness can be replaced with something else.

I wanted to be helpful. "Can I do anything else? I'll make all the calls and I'll get everything in order here, but can I do anything for you? Can I bring you anything?"

She paused, and I thought she was going to say no, tell me to do the work and just go home, that she didn't need me.

"We're at Saint Mary's. Stop by here later if you want." She managed to surprise me. "Right now it's just my brothers and me. Dad's sleeping. He's probably going to sleep until the doctor comes to see him again. Bring some whiskey and a six-pack if you want. The boys, not my dad, would probably appreciate it." I liked that she wanted my help. It made me feel useful.

I busied myself with calling all the numbers on both the lists and telling them about what happened to Eddie. The amount of goodwill on the other line was astonishing but not surprising. No one seemed to mind about losing a few days' work or a few days' fish. All anyone wanted to know was what they could do to help Eddie and Kit.

I spent a couple of hours on the phone, straightened up the office, and shut the window, then went out to make sure all the boats were secure before realizing I had no way to get to the hospital since I drove my boat to the docks every day. I wandered back into the office, pulled a dusty yellow pages off the shelf and thumbed through it to find the North Fork cab company. Thankfully I had a few twenties and my driver's license in a paper clip in my pocket. I hated carrying my entire wallet out on the boat, for fear it would slip out and I'd have to replace everything, but at least I had remembered to bring this. It took the cabbie almost an hour to get to me, and then I had to direct him to the nearest liquor store and then onto Saint Mary's. I wished I'd been able to stop and get some food for them, but for now this was the best I could do.

The woman at the information desk in the hospital looked like she might be asleep, so I faked a sneeze in order to startle her and asked what room Eddie Delgado was in. In a wheezy voice she told me to go to the fourth floor and ask the attending nurse.

I could hear a low chuckle that I recognized as Eddie's when I got off the elevator. I followed the sound to a small private room with a view of the water and then lingered outside the door. Both of the Delgado boys perched on the edge of their father's bed as he told them a story that seemed to involve getting into a fight with Bruce Springsteen's bass player or maybe getting onstage somewhere with Bruce Springsteen's bass player. Both of Eddie's sons were big guys, linebacker big. One had a shaved head with a tattoo of a badger curled over his naked ear. The other had the most glorious head of hair I had ever seen on anyone outside of a game-show host.

"Shut up, man. Man, you're a fibber," the one with the glorious hair said.

"I've seen you play the bass, and it sounded like a cow got tipped over and given an enema," the other one howled.

"Don't make me laugh, Larry," Eddie said. "You'll give me another heart attack."

I watched as the two men clucked over their dad, tucking a blanket around his feet, placing a pillow behind his back. And they laughed. Laughter that was real and honest. I couldn't imagine a scene even close to this with my father. He had only ever been in the hospital once that I remembered. I was ten. It was the year he'd gotten very into long-distance cycling. That was also the year my mother learned she wasn't going to be able to have any more children besides me. I wasn't supposed to know that, but I did. I had always listened carefully to my mother's conversations, desperate to know what was happening, to know how I could make her happier on the days when she seemed so sad. In hindsight I wondered if the two things, my father's biking and my mother's discovery, were at all correlated, not cause and effect correlated, but maybe my dad needed his own escape from us and that escape was long-distance biking. My mother's escape seemed to be throwing herself into her board meetings and gala planning, stuffing her sadness down inside of her. I never even saw her cry. Dad had trained for six months to do his century ride, a one-hundred-mile ride from Manhattan to the tip of Montauk on a road bike. He'd hardly made it out of Queens before he was sideswiped by a mail truck. We got taken to the hospital in Hempstead, but my mother immediately sent me home with the nanny the second we walked into my father's room and saw him hooked up to an IV and a couple of other tubes and wires.

"We don't want to upset Henry. This is too upsetting," I remembered her saying.

How many situations had I been kept from for fear that they would upset me?

Kit was curled into a chair in the corner, looking even smaller next to her massive siblings. I gave a weak knock on the doorframe to announce myself.

"Who are you?" The one with the tattoo turned to look at me. Kit managed a small smile when she saw me.

"Did you let everyone know?"

"Let everyone know what?" Eddie asked.

Kit answered for me. "I asked Joe to make a few phone calls and let people know you would be out of commission for a couple of days," Kit said it warily, like she was preparing for an argument.

"I'm fine."

"You're not." She said it more surely and looked at me. "Everyone is okay? No one is pissed?"

"Everyone is okay," I said.

"Get in here," Eddie boomed. "Come on, Joe. Don't be shy."

"This is Joe." He introduced me to his sons. "Joe's been helping me out this summer. When I first got ahold of him he couldn't tell which way was the eel's eye and which was its asshole, but now he's my best guy. My very best guy."

It wasn't true, but it touched me all the same. I thought about what my own dad had said to me at my Princeton graduation. "As expected, Henry. As expected."

"You're a good teacher," I mumbled.

Maybe Kit could sense my embarrassment. "Dad needs rest," she insisted then to the entire room. "He needs to take a nap, and he needs to take one now, so why don't I drive everyone back to the house for a little while."

They agreed, and soon the four of us were in Kit's tiny car with Bruce Springsteen blaring from the CD player. The three of them knew every lyric to "Thunder Road." Larry made his hand into a fist and thrust it like a microphone in front of my lips. I mumbled nonsense into it, wishing I was cooler and knew all the lyrics to all the Bruce Springsteen songs.

Larry didn't care. He took on the next verse. "'Well now, I'm no hero, that's understood.'" He had a pretty decent voice. I told him so, and he punched me in the arm hard enough to leave a bruise.

When Kit dropped her brothers off at Eddie's house she asked me to move up to the front seat.

"So I don't feel like your chauffeur," she insisted. "Can I take you back to your boat? I really appreciate you making those calls and coming by the hospital."

I realized as I climbed over the bag of booze to get to the front that I'd forgotten to give it to Kit's brothers.

"Should we go back to give it to them?"

"Nah," she said, shaking her head. "They'll figure something out. They always do. I'll keep it." She rubbed at her eyes with the tips of her index fingers. "I could use a drink."

"I don't need to get back right away. I can stick around for a while."

"Want to come over? We can drink a couple of those beers?"

I nodded and turned the music down so we could maybe talk, but Kit turned it right back up so loud we wouldn't be able to hear each other.

Her apartment was a few blocks from her office, right on the town's main drag, over the general store. The wooden stairs to her place were around the back and wobbled as we climbed them. She lived in a small one-bedroom, but the living room contained a large bay window on its east side with a view over the shorter buildings across the street and right out to the water.

Kit motioned to it. "Not a bad selling point."

"Not at all. But you can see your office from your living room."

"And from my bathroom, actually."

The walls were painted a cheery yellow, covered in pictures of her with her dad and brothers. I was mesmerized by the timeline of adorable little Kit growing into a woman, dancing on the boat, stern and focused in a Little League photo, laughing with her head thrown back on her dad's shoulders. She startled me when she plunked the grocery bag down on the small linoleum kitchen table that separated the kitchenette from the living area.

"Beer or whiskey?"

"What are you having?"

"I think I need a whiskey."

"Same, then."

Kit opened a well-organized cabinet and pulled out over-whelmingly adult glassware that looked like something in my mother's kitchen and went about fixing us a cocktail well beyond a simple water and whiskey. She added bitters and syrup like a real bartender and even shook it up in a fancy-looking copper shaker.

"So," I started before she sat down, "how bad was it?"

A bird landed on the ledge outside the big window, and Kit stared at it for a second before she answered. "I know it didn't look too awful in there today, but I found him crumpled on the floor when I went to his house last night, curled up in the fetal position. He didn't know what was happening, and he was barely conscious." She took a sip of her drink that finished half her glass. "Thankfully the ambulance got there in less than fifteen minutes, and the doctor saw him right away and they were able to stabilize him. But it was touch and go, and it was just him and me. My brothers didn't get in until after midnight, and I just sat there thinking, *This is it.* I knew he was going to die. Right then." Her voice cracked and she stopped. I held her hand in silence while we both finished our drinks. When the glasses were empty I refilled them without asking.

"What did they say was wrong with him?" I asked carefully.

"Oh, it was definitely a heart attack. No one was surprised by that. They injected something into his heart that helped remove the clot that was blocking everything up, and that saved him. But it's gonna happen again. And he needs this surgery. An angleplasty . . . I think they called it that. No, that's wrong. An angioplasty to make sure the blood can keep getting to his heart." Her cheeks were slick with tears. Displays of emotion like that made me nervous, but I found myself scooting closer to her so I could sling a comforting arm around her shoulders. In that moment I would give anything to try to make it better for her. I wanted to hold her like that for as long as she'd let me.

"He's going to be okay. That's a pretty routine surgery, and it's usually successful." I had no idea if that was true, but I wanted to give her hope.

But she didn't answer.

"Or maybe not," she finally said, swiping away the tears and snot.

Crying doesn't do much for most girls, but it made Kit even prettier. Maybe it's because it was the first time I'd ever seen her vulnerable.

"We can't afford the surgery anyway. He doesn't have any health insurance. Neither of us do. We let the payments lapse too long. I told him we couldn't do that, and he promised we would get it all straightened out in September, but that will be too late."

I'd never even thought twice about insurance, and that realization warmed my neck and cheeks with shame.

She must have seen the crimson hue to my cheeks. "No one ever thinks about these kinds of things until they smack us in the face. You never think the worst is really gonna happen."

"What are you going to do?"

"I honestly don't know. We would need to sell a couple of the boats to come up with that kind of money. It's more than fifty thousand dollars from what I can tell. Plus this hospital stay . . . whatever that costs." She put her forehead down on the table, let it bang down on the hard surface. "I tried to talk to him about it. He won't sell anything. We barely make the margins with the number of boats we have right now."

"What do your brothers say?"

"They don't have any money. Larry's got two kids. Jimmy lives in a one-bedroom apartment with three guys on Avenue D, dreaming of becoming Cher's hairdresser."

"What about your dad's house?"

She got quiet.

"I thought there might be money in the house, but he took a line of credit on it already. How did I let it get this bad?" she said.

"It's not your fault," I told her. "It's not. You've done your best." I grew bolder and placed my hand on her damp cheek. "You're doing great."

"I should have pushed him to start selling things off a year ago."

"You couldn't have known this would happen."

"We can't sell anything fast enough right now. No bank is gonna give us a loan. I don't even know anyone who has any money that I could ask to borrow it from."

I have it! I could give it to you.

I almost told her everything right then. I almost told her that there had to be some way I could get the money for her. I opened my mouth, and my jaw hung there dumbly, mute. The fact that I couldn't tell her after all that made me a goddamn coward. I was terrified of what she would say to me when she learned my secret, terrified she would tell me to get the hell out of her cozy little apartment and never come back. I was terrified I would never see her again.

So instead I hugged her closer, feeling her small ribs flutter against mine like the wings of a frightened butterfly.

"You can do this. You can raise the money. I'll help." I started to tell her about all the phone calls I'd made that morning, about how everyone wanted to help Eddie, how beloved he was. I could tell it made her feel a little bit better, even if she didn't believe I'd found some grand solution to the problem. Her breathing got more even, and she finally relaxed against me. I lowered my lips to her forehead. Her skin was warm on my mouth.

"Can we put on some music?" she asked. "Something he'd like."

I found *The Stranger* on her CD rack and put on "Scenes from an Italian Restaurant" as she mixed us our third drinks. I hadn't eaten anything all day. She probably hadn't either.

"Want to go to Martha's?" I asked. "My treat."

She shook her head, quietly singing to herself. "'Eddie could never afford to live that kind of life. . . .They started to fight when the money got tight, and they just didn't count on the tears.'"

I'd heard Eddie sing that song at least a dozen times on the boat, but it took on a new sadness when Kit sang it.

By the end of the song Brenda and Eddie had split up, Kit was back on the couch next to me, and we were halfway through a glass of whiskey neither of us needed.

"All I could think about was that I was disappointing him." Kit slurred a little. "That by staying here and taking care of him I wasn't living up to what he might want me to do. I've never thought about that before."

"I don't think you're disappointing him. I think he just wants you to be happy. It's what all parents want for their kids." I was one to talk about parents and the things we did to please them.

"When he gets better I'm gonna do something. Something different."

She kissed me first. It's a little fuzzy, but I know that much.

It was a desperate kiss, the kiss of someone who does it because they want to feel something else. But I did kiss her back, tentatively at first. I wanted to comfort her, protect her, and this was what she needed. At some point we moved to her bedroom. The sun was just beginning to set, and it was still light. We fumbled a little like uncertain strangers. It could have been because we were heading toward the sloppier side of drunk, but I think it was because neither of us knew if we truly wanted to commit to what was about to happen. I was terrified to cross a line with her.

But what happened next was simple and sweet. We both kept our eyes closed, our lips faintly touching the entire time. It didn't last very long, but by the time it was over we were both exhausted, physically and emotionally. I don't want to say much else about it. I don't think she'd want me to.

We both fell asleep. I woke up before she did. It was pitch-black in the apartment, and my head was pounding. She was so content lying there, and my feelings were in such a confusing tangle that I thought it might be best if I left without waking her up.

My shirt was in the kitchen, my shorts had somehow found their way under her bed. I put them on quickly and then tucked the flowered comforter around her small body, hovering over her for a moment. I risked tucking a piece of hair behind her delicate ear and kissing her again on the forehead before I walked out the door.

CHAPTER THIRTEEN

I could fix this. That's all I could think about as I made my way back across the bay. I made plans and did the math to keep my emotions in check. I knew there was approximately $35,000 in my savings account accumulated from various birthday and Christmas presents and a modest inheritance from a great-aunt I'd never met. I'd gotten a couple of bonds when I was ten years old that might have come due, but figuring out the logistics of selling bonds seemed too complicated. My watch, a gift from my father for my graduation day, was worth at least $10,000 new, but who knew what I could get for it used or how I would even sell it anyway. Even if I could find one, I didn't have the balls to just walk into a pawnshop.

During the moments when I stopped making plans I felt a little disgusted with myself. How could I have just left her there? I should have stuck around after spending the night with her, but I couldn't face Kit when she woke up. I couldn't stand the thought of trying to comfort her—sober, in the light of day—and telling her everything would be all right, that I would be there for her. That would have been worse than all the lies I'd already told her. Everything wasn't going to be all right. Eddie would die if he didn't get the surgery. And I wouldn't be there for her. The person she'd slept with didn't even exist. In less than a month I'd be back in Manhattan, working nine to nine, collecting a good paycheck and health insurance. She didn't even know my real name. I was a phony and a fraud.

I couldn't face her until I could do something real to help her.

There was only one thing in my possession that I knew was worth something and that I actually knew how to sell—a first edition of William Faulkner's *Go Down, Moses*, with its red cloth cover in immaculate condition. The book was worth at least $15,000. I knew that because Truman, the curator at my father's favorite rare bookshop on East Fifty-Seventh, was always asking him about it when we went in. The book had been a gift to my father and then a regift to me on my sixteenth birthday. Originally published as a collection of short stories, the book can also read like a novel, and I liked that about it, the fact that it could be something different to different people. But I knew my father didn't love Faulkner, and I always wondered if that was why he gave it to me. I knew the books he loved, all the first editions of Hemingways and Fitzgeralds that he kept under lock and key. The Faulkner, for all its value, was always something of an afterthought for him. It was currently in my childhood bedroom, just a few hours away. If I sold that book and drained my savings account I could pay for Eddie's surgery.

In the end what would it really trouble me? I'd gladly do it if it could save Eddie. Not just for Kit, but because of everything that man had given me in the past couple of months—a new perspective on the world, a useful skill.

The problem was Truman. That guy was a talker, a storyteller, a gossip, and there was no way he'd keep quiet about me coming to sell my Faulkner to him. But there had been several hundred copies published. It wasn't like I had the only copy in existence.

Someone could go into that store and sell the Faulkner. It just couldn't be me.

"So you're telling me that book is worth fifteen K?" Sperry asked me. He sat up in bed and rubbed his eyes. Mrs. Frankweiler was curled into a C on his bare belly. She gazed at me with her old-soul eyes and then promptly yawned.

"I think so, man. Or maybe more," I said through my own yawn, trying to act casual about it. I'd taken the boat home in the dark and allowed myself a couple of hours of sleep and a few more of lying in bed and staring at the ceiling trying to figure out how to come up with the remaining balance of cash.

"Why are you selling it? Are you in trouble? Did you get someone pregnant? She can't prove it right away, you know. You have to wait until the baby's actually born. There's no rush."

"No one is pregnant."

"Then why do you need all that cash?" Sperry cast a concerned look my way. "Drugs? Rehab?"

"We don't live in an after-school special. No pregnancy. No drugs. A friend of mine needs a loan . . . for a medical procedure."

"Plastic surgery?"

"Heart surgery."

Sperry considered the gravity of heart surgery for a moment.

"So if I sell this old book for you . . . can I wear a disguise?"

"If you really want to."

"I definitely want to wear a disguise. I've got this fake mustache I've been dying to try out."

I couldn't find my driver's license, but my passport was enough to get a cashier's check with the money from my savings account.

The bank issued me a second one with the $17,000 that Truman had offered Sperry for the Faulkner.

"The guy practically had a hard-on when I told him I wanted to sell him that book," Sperry said when he got back the next day, still wearing a costume-store mustache and a bright blue Mets hats so that he looked a little bit like Keith Hernandez trying to wear a Keith Hernandez disguise.

Instead of taking the boat, I drove to the North Fork for the first time all summer, my heart pounding the entire way. Kit wasn't at the office or her apartment. I was hoping to avoid a scene at the hospital, but I didn't know how else to get her the money in time.

In the lobby, I paused in front of the gift shop. Should I get her some chocolates? Something nice. It felt like the right thing to do, but all they had inside were some peanut M&M's and Snickers bars. I grabbed a bouquet of wilted daisies instead.

Thankfully Eddie was asleep when I arrived. There she was. Sweet Kit, curled up in that same chair in the corner, her legs tucked beneath her like a child. I thought back to one of the pictures on the wall in her apartment, her standing on the beach in a black-and-white polka-dot one-piece bathing suit holding up a fish as long as her arm, laughing wildly with her head thrown back in glee. I'd do anything to make her that happy again.

Tucked in the chair, her clothes looked clean but rumpled, like she'd slept in that exact position, in that exact same outfit. She didn't smile when she looked up and saw me. Instead, her face contorted into something else entirely, a frown, a grimace, and then a flash of anger. I never should have left her like that. I should have stayed until the morning. We should have talked. I'd have to own up to that now, before I even gave her the money. I needed to start being a man about my mistakes.

"Can we go outside?" I asked, holding out the sad, limp daisies. Her only response was a curt nod. Kit took the flowers from me and placed them on the tray next to Eddie's bed, not even bothering to get them some water. We rode the elevator in silence. A doctor and nurse got on at the second floor, but they decided to ignore each other too. Once we were outside the hospital's revolving doors, Kit pulled out a crumpled pack of Kools and a lighter. She didn't offer me one.

There was no use waiting.

"I shouldn't have left. I'm sorry I left," I blurted out.

"I don't want to talk about that." Her voice held a warning.

I switched gears then. "I have the money for you. I was able to borrow it. It wasn't easy, but I've got it. It's enough for Eddie to get the surgery." Once I said it, I knew how strange it sounded. I should have practiced what I was going to say to her, or maybe written her a letter alongside the checks and then talked to her afterward.

She just stared at me. There wasn't even a flicker of confusion on her face. She lit the cigarette and took in a long pull.

I began to babble like an idiot. "It wasn't a big problem. I want you to have it. You don't have to pay it back."

She exhaled smoke and when she spoke her voice was dripping in sarcasm. "That's very kind of you, Henry."

Henry. I took a step back. She knew. How did she know? My hands went slick. I felt a wave of nausea start in my stomach and creep up into my throat.

My vision blurred, and I could hardly see Kit fumbling in her purse, reaching out a hand to me with something in it.

"I think this belongs to you," she said in a voice as cold as ice.

My money clip. My driver's license. My real name. My real

address. Henry Cane. East Eighty-Third Street. I knew then that it must have fallen out of my shorts at her apartment.

"You have a mighty fancy address, Henry Cane," she said. "It's been a while since I've been to the city, but I know the son of a plumber doesn't live on a street like that. And I don't think Michigan is so close to Central Park. Tell me the truth."

I swallowed back the bile rising in my throat. Every muscle in my body tightened, and my heart clanged against my ribs. I wanted to turn and run away from her, from this situation. I'd grown so accustomed to lying, I no longer knew how to tell the truth.

"I can explain," I sputtered stupidly.

Kit knew what to say. She was enraged. "Explain that you decided to spend the summer slumming it with us? That you thought it would be fun to get your hands dirty for a little while? Bang some working-class girl . . . then swoop in with all your money and be a hero?" She took a drag of her cigarette. "I don't need to hear *that* explanation. And I don't need your money."

She had to take the money. She had to. It was the only thing I had to give her.

"You do. Please, please take it. Please." I insisted, I begged. "Eddie needs it. He doesn't need to know where it came from. Tell him it was donated by all the guys, all the folks in town. Tell him it was anonymous. Don't tell him anything, but get your father that surgery."

She kept glaring at me. "Did you have fun pretending to be poor, Henry?"

I tried to get the words out through the tightness in my chest. "I wasn't trying to pretend to be anything. I just wanted a job."

"And what about all the other things you told me? Your hopes and dreams. You want to be a writer some day . . ." She almost spat when she said the word *writer*. "Who the hell are you?"

An elderly couple hobbling toward the hospital entrance paused to watch us. A crew of orderlies stopped their small talk and just stared. I tried to pull Kit farther into the parking lot, but she shrugged me away. "That was true. Is true. I didn't lie to you about anything except my name and where I was from."

I could feel every set of eyes in the parking lot on us. I hated having an audience, hated being watched. I hated what I'd done to her. I hated myself.

"Please take the check, Kit. Eddie would want you to."

"How do you know what my father would want? You don't know him. And we don't know you. Who the hell are you? Do you work for one of the big fishing companies? Did you come out here to check us out? Well, we aren't much competition now."

I shook my head, but only managed one word. "No."

Tears welled in her eyes—I wasn't sure if she was breaking or if they were tears of rage. She tossed her cigarette on the ground, stubbed the cherry out with the toe of her sneaker. She bit her wobbly lower lip. I reached out to pull her toward me, and for a minute she let me hold her. I buried my face in her hair, inhaling her scent of smoke and Ivory soap.

"You're wonderful," I whispered. It was something I should have told her the other night, because it was true. She *was* wonderful. "You're a good daughter, and you love him so much. I know you want to take care of him, and you have been doing a great job, but someone has to help you. Someone has to take care of you. Your dad loves you. I know he loves his business and the people who work for him, and I know he doesn't want all of you to go bankrupt to take care of him. He will do anything to make sure he doesn't disappoint you. Look. You can think I'm a rich asshole all you want. Maybe you're right. But take the check."

"You don't know him."

"I'm right, Kit."

She pulled away from me and stared right through me. I felt like a small child. I was surprised when she finally reached over for the checks. She clasped at the two pieces of paper, glanced at them for a brief moment, and slid them into the back pocket of her jean shorts.

What she said next sliced me so deep I knew I would never forget it. "You don't want to take care of me, Henry," she said. "You just wanted to play the hero for a little while, to pretend to be someone else because maybe you don't like who you really are."

CHAPTER FOURTEEN

The best summer of my life was all a lie.

I could never go back to Greenport again, never show my face to Eddie or Kit. I had this whole other house of cards built with Elisabetta—one that had *real* consequences for my *real* life, for my father's business. Kit was right. I had been burying my real life inside of another. I was a coward.

I did what a coward would do. I roamed the house aimlessly for days, sleeping sporadically, hardly eating, a regular Miss Havisham in the body of a lanky man-child. To his credit, Sperry excelled at taking care of me. He seemed to know that I needed to get blind drunk that first night, so he pulled out a bottle of my father's Ballantine's and we went to work. In the morning he cooked me a feast of scrambled eggs and extra crispy bacon and then let me go back to sleep. We spent an entire day on the couch eating chips, Cheetos, and some fancy, stinky cheese my mother had left in the fridge. We sat still for so long that when I finally rose to pee my legs were filled with pins and needles. The drinking started again shortly after sunset. At some point during the night the entire story began to pour out of me—Kit, Eddie, Elisabetta.

"So you're telling me that you blew off an entire summer of pussy hunting with me to get your Mrs. Robinson on?"

I didn't have the energy to deal with Sperry's misogyny right then, but I should have gotten together a well-thought-out diatribe on why pussy hunting was neither appropriate to say or correct grammar, for that matter. "I wouldn't exactly put it like that," I said instead.

After hearing my story about Elisabetta, Sperry did kind of look at me with a newfound respect. He let me mope for the next forty-eight hours before he decided to kick my ass into some kind of action, focusing first on Sam Hartwell and his novel.

"You need to get that book, man," he said as he fixed us mimosas on the sunporch. "It would be a huge coup. You'd go into that new job with balls the size of a Bentley."

Balls that big sounded painful. "It could all be a moot point. I don't even know if he's sold it yet." I dumped the cocktail into a nearby potted plant and poured my glass full of orange juice when Sperry wasn't looking.

"Well, find out. Don't be such a pussy about it."

I couldn't let it go again. The word crept under my skin like a tick. "If you say that word again I'm making you go back to live with your stepmom."

"Yeah, yeah, yeah. Don't be such a vagina. Is that better?"

"No."

"Anyway," he huffed. "We're going to do some investigating. Find out whether he's sold that book. This is going to be your life in less than a month. Jump in. Embrace it." It was incredibly disconcerting for Sperry to be the voice of reason in any situation. "The hot wife would probably help you. She likes you. Hates her husband. Don't you think she'd do you a solid?"

The truth was, I had absolutely no idea. Like Kit, Elisabetta had no idea who I really was. And even if she did, why would she help me? Who was I to her? But Sperry was right. My life was in publishing, and despite everything I'd done to the contrary all summer, I wanted to make my father proud; I wanted to do a good job.

"I'll try to find out about the book."

Sarah Knowles worked out of a small office her husband had built for her on the edge of their property in Amagansett. The three-hundred-square-foot room had floor-to-ceiling windows overlooking white sandy dunes.

"You know what they say about people in glass houses." She winked when she opened the door to let me inside. Her hair was wet, and she wore what looked like the kind of thing my mother threw on over her bathing suits. It was hot pink with fluorescent green elephants marching obediently across it. In any other setting it might have been called trashy, but poolside in the Hamptons these kinds of clothes seemed to make a peculiar kind of sense.

If she was taken aback by my unruly beard and disheveled appearance she didn't bat an eye.

"Do you want a water . . . or a gin and tonic? Those are truly the only beverages I keep back here," she insisted in a high, tinkly voice. "You're over twenty-one now. I don't think your mother would disapprove." I'd studied my parents' friends for most of my life, trying to crack their codes so that one day when I grew up, I would know how to be like them. They terrified me with their formalities, their secret language, but watching them was a comfort. They gave me clues. It was all something I could learn. When

Sarah Knowles offered me a gin and tonic I felt like I'd finally crossed some imaginary threshold.

I accepted the water instead of the cocktail and sat on a wide green velvet couch covered in throw pillows. I couldn't figure out how to sit on that couch. It was too wide and too deep with way too many cushions. I perched precariously on the edge, which forced my knees to knock unpleasantly together.

"Thanks for letting me come over, Mrs. Knowles." I'd called that morning and asked if we could chat about an article she'd written about a surfing Buddhist monk who lived out at Montauk. I said something about how I thought he might have a memoir in him. It was a flimsy excuse at best. She didn't seem to care, so long as I was keeping her company.

She laughed into her highball glass. "You know you can call me Sarah."

We briefly attempted small talk. She regaled me with tales of her daughter, Astrid, a premed student taking a year off to do something with some kind of nonprofit in Africa. Sarah couldn't remember which country. I'd once had a crush on Astrid—she was my first kiss. Her mouth had tasted like pink Trident and the warm white wine spritzer she stole from her parents. But after this summer that time felt like eons ago, like a different Henry Cane had lived that reality.

"Africa is a big place." I tried to sound apologetic and understanding about the fact that she couldn't remember where her daughter was volunteering, but it still felt a little ridiculous. I'd been to Kenya two summers ago to help my mother with her latest charitable project, an initiative that recycles old books into building materials that can be used to make schools for girls. I'd been so inspired I hadn't wanted to leave.

"It's Tanzania." She snapped her fingers. "I knew I knew it. I was going to say Zanzibar, but I knew that wasn't right. Zanzibar is all beaches and Maasai, and Tanzania is safari and Maasai. Silly me. I should know better." She sipped her drink. "So are you ready to start your big job in a few weeks?"

She reached over to rub her ankle. I thought about Elisabetta's description of her. She did have legs like a giraffe, long and spindly, almost buckling at the knees when she stood to get herself more ice, as if the meager weight of her torso was too much to bear. In my mind I compared her legs to Elisabetta's, which were sleek and muscular, tanned but not worn. God, even with everything happening with Kit and with Eddie, I couldn't get Elisabetta out of my mind. Maybe I wanted her even more than before, needed her more. I kept thinking how easy it would be to lose myself, to dull my pain with just a few hours in her bed. I didn't know if it was love or obsession or a dangerous combination of the two.

"I'm getting there." I tried to affect an easy nonchalance. "I'm excited to get started working with the writers. I have some leads on a couple of really interesting debuts, and of course everyone is talking about the Sam Hartwell novel." This was the reason I'd come. If anyone knew anything about Sam Hartwell's novel it would be Sarah Knowles.

That caught her interest. "Of course. What have you heard about it?"

"I probably don't know much more than you do. In fact, you probably know more. You always know more." Flattery helped with women like Sarah Knowles.

She leaned back in her chair. "I honestly don't know that much. The drafts of the novel have been under lock and key. Everyone wants it. Including your father. I told your mother to try to use some of her charm with Elisabetta. Elisabetta just adores your mother."

My stomach lurched at the idea of my mother and Elisabetta even living on the same planet, breathing the same air. To me they inhabited two entirely distinct worlds. The knowledge that they had ever even crossed paths made the air in the room feel thicker, like we were wading through something we wouldn't be able to wash off. "Maybe I will have one of those gin and tonics," I said. "I didn't know my mother and Elisabetta knew each other."

It wasn't like I kept tabs on all my mother's friends. That would be impossible. She was a woman who befriended a seatmate on every single plane ride she'd ever taken, who attracted new people to her like flies to an open jar of jam. But this was different. I felt like I would have known if she was friends with Sam Hartwell's beautiful and esoteric Italian wife. For a moment, I considered the source, knowing that Sarah Knowles was prone to hyperbole. I couldn't imagine my mother as the kind of woman Elisabetta would like spending time with, particularly after how much she seemed to dislike Sarah Knowles.

"I think they met a few years ago in Rome," she went on, much to my dismay. "Or maybe it was Florence. You must think I'm terrible with geography, but when you travel as much as we do it really is hard to keep track. But I do know that Elisabetta took her out to the Chianti wine region. Yes, definitely. Your mother shipped a case to me for my birthday, and we finished the last bottle recently."

"How fun," I managed. "I don't think I knew about that trip. Was Sam with them?"

"I don't know if Sam went—I don't think your father went. He had to be at some conference. He's always at some conference.

But it sounded like your mother and Elisabetta had a delightful time. Your mother has a delightful time everywhere she goes though. I think they've met up during a few other trips."

I tried to picture it. My mother and Elisabetta driving the winding roads of Tuscany, sipping thick red wine together and laughing about their ridiculous husbands like they were characters in a movie. It felt impossible.

Sarah poured me a stiff drink. "This gin comes from this small distillery up the Hudson. We adore it up there. Hastings? Such a quaint town. I keep telling Bob that we should sell the place on Madison and live between there and here, but he hates the commute. Says the train smells like feet."

"It is absolutely lovely there," I agreed. Part of me hoped if I had a drink she would have another and that it would loosen her and she'd keep telling me more. She did pour herself a second glass, but I had to nudge her a little.

"What about the book? What are people saying about the book? I'm personally excited for it. I was a huge *Desolation Wilderness* fan."

"Well." She paused to let me know she was about to tell me something that wasn't common knowledge. Sarah Knowles needed an audience, loved an audience. "I hear Hartwell doesn't even care about the money. He's been living off the residuals from *Desolation Wilderness* his entire life. That movie though . . . it was terrible, right?"

I had almost forgotten that *Desolation Wilderness* had been turned into a movie. I was young when it came out in the early eighties. I remembered that it was nominated for a lot of awards and critics loved it, but most people who had seen it decried it as dull, slow art-house slop. Still, it starred a lot of people who were very famous before I was born, and I imagined that it made him an awful lot of money, enough to travel the world with his beautiful wife and then rent her an old Victorian on Shelter Island.

"Terrible," I agreed.

"He also makes a fair amount off speaking fees. I won't even tell you what we ended up paying him to come to the Whole Love event. Your mother said she could probably convince him to do it for free, as a friend, but that agent of his was relentless. Anyway. I heard he doesn't care about a bidding war. He wants to find the perfect editor, someone who gets him. He's calling it his life's greatest work." She rolled her eyes as if to mock the kind of man who called anything their "life's greatest work" and swirled the remnants of ice around in her glass so that they made a pleasant clanking sound.

"What about his wife?" Once it was out of my mouth, I didn't know why I had said it. It was a complete non sequitur.

"What about her?"

"I was just curious what she thought of the whole thing, of being out here for the summer, of him writing all the time in the city."

"I'm doing a story on her, you know. For *Vanity Fair* actually. She's quite a famous artist in Italy. It's not the kind of work I enjoy. Very abstract, but the Europeans seem to like it. They're quite an interesting couple. I've been spending a lot of time with them for this piece. Their connection is quite interesting. Electric almost."

Of course I knew Elisabetta was an artist, all those half-finished canvases all over the house. But a famous one? How many secrets were we both keeping from each other?

"What do you mean?"

"He just seems to depend on her so much, and they've been together for so long. They met when she was a teenage model. Right after he published *Desolation Wilderness*. She quit her modeling career shortly after they got married though. She doesn't seem like the type who would enjoy modeling much anyway. She's so cerebral."

Sarah Knowles, for all of her powers of gossip and information, was getting it all wrong. Elisabetta couldn't stand her husband. She was trapped in that marriage. It was a terrible marriage.

The gin was starting to make me nauseous, and I suddenly regretted coming to see this woman. I'd found out exactly what I had wanted to know. The book was still available. I still had a chance of getting it. I just had to figure out how to confess to Elisabetta, had to figure out whether she would help me. And more than that I had to do what might be one of the hardest things I'd ever done in my entire life. I'd have to say goodbye to her.

I could tell that Sarah Knowles wanted me to keep asking her questions. "I think I need to head home now. I promised Sperry I would meet him for dinner at Duryea's."

"So far. Such a drive." She said it like Montauk was in New Jersey. "Of course. How is Brett doing? How is he holding up? This is his father's fifth divorce, no?"

This was the problem with talking to Sarah Knowles. She'd always give you a little something, but she always wanted something in return.

"I don't think the divorce is official. They're separated. Sperry is fine."

"He's used to it by now," she said with an expression of faux sadness and empathy. "He's a good boy, Brett. High-spirited. Could still stand to lose a few pounds. But he'll do just fine working with his father."

"He will. I really need to go meet him, Mrs. Knowles. He's actually been a little broken up lately. Not about the divorce. But, you know, he broke up with Posie Montague."

She raised her eyebrows a fraction of a centimeter at the new information. I'd given her only a small something, but it was still something. Sarah Knowles smiled, her mouth fluffed into a perpetual pout that would have been adorable on a toddler.

"Thanks again for the drink," I said, standing.

She put her hand on my shoulder. "You and Astrid should really get together when she comes home from Zanzibar . . . or Tanzania." She looked me up and down, assessing a young man she thought she knew. I hardly knew him myself. "You really are quite a catch, Henry Cane."

CHAPTER FIFTEEN

The check cleared.

But it had been a week and Kit still hadn't called me back. Maybe she'd never call me back and I would have to find a way to be okay with it. But that possibility didn't seem real to me. I couldn't imagine never speaking to her again, never knowing if she was okay.

I left a message on Eddie's office's answering machine to say I wouldn't be working the boats anymore. What kind of goddamn coward quits his job on someone's answering machine?

When my account balance dropped to nearly zero, I should have been terrified, but I wasn't. It was a good feeling, the rare feeling of having done the right thing. I needed that feeling amid the morass of having done so many wrong things.

You just wanted to play the hero. Kit's words echoed through my head for days.

I'd never been a hero, not even in my own story.

I realized more and more that I'd come across as more of a supporting character, not even the sidekick, but someone ancillary to the plot. I was the guy you forget about five minutes after he'd left the screen. I was more like the guy who marries Carrie Fisher in *When Harry Met Sally* and gets his wagon-wheel coffee table thrown to the curb. Who remembers that guy's name? No-body. He married Princess freaking Leia and nobody ever remem-bers his name.

No, I was never the hero. Maybe I was never meant to be.

After more days of wallowing in the house, reading old Agatha Christie novels, and subsisting on cheese sandwiches and beer, Sperry asked me to take him fishing. A lifetime of living near the water and, like me, he'd hardly picked up a pole, and now that I was an expert he wanted me to show him what I'd learned.

"Real men hunt their food." He beat on his chest with his hands clenched into thick fists, his gold signet ring catching the sun.

I had to admit I was also itching to get back on the water.

"I don't have my own equipment." Everything I'd ever used to fish had belonged to Eddie.

"Tell me what we need," he'd insisted. "I'll take care of every-thing."

That's how we ended up with more than a grand's worth of brand-new fishing gear, half of which we didn't need but the guy at the bait and tackle shop could tell Sperry was an easy target and even managed to sell him a pair of "fishing gloves." Kit would have died hearing about that.

Hooking eels came easily to Sperry. And actually, his shiny latex gloves didn't hurt. Though most things came easily to Sperry. I'd learned a long time ago that he could mimic almost anyone and any task. Maybe I'd always envied him over it.

"This is disgusting and marvelous," he announced as his first piece of bait dangled off the end of his line. "Look at us. A couple of modern-day Ahabs."

I didn't bother to tell him that Ahab, a one-legged, revenge-driven sociopath, wasn't exactly an aspirational character. I'd always preferred the whale. I slung an arm around his shoulder and said, "Good job, man. You're a natural."

It turned out to be this great day, probably one of the better days Sperry and I had since we outgrew Wiffle ball, fort building, and farting on each other's heads. We nursed a six-pack and then another and sipped on a fifth of whiskey. It was a lazy day and we were preoccupied with the fishing, so we didn't feel that drunk until the sun began to set.

I started to pack up all his new gear. We'd been successful enough, catching a couple of flounder and throwing them on ice in the small cooler. Sperry wanted to know how to gut them and clean them so he could put them on the grill later, but it was a skill I had yet to learn, and I said we'd have to get them home and then figure something out. I had a feeling there was someone we could hire to come to our house, gut our fish, and toss them with a bit of lemon and cilantro. There were few services you couldn't order up on demand in our part of the Hamptons.

"Did you see your girl?" Sperry slurred. "This week. Have you seen her?"

It was funny to hear Elisabetta referred to as a girl, let alone *my* girl, when she was anything but. Annie had been a girl. Caroline had been a girl. Kit was a girl. And maybe a part of them, big or small, had belonged to me. But certainly not Elisabetta. She was something else entirely. The answer was no. I'd passed the house a few times, but the scarf was never there, and a part of me wondered if she'd left without saying goodbye. Then again, how could she say goodbye? She didn't even know my real name.

"I haven't seen her" is all I said. Sperry chattered excitedly, and

I took a long gulp of the whiskey, finishing off the bottle, letting my head go a little hazy.

I looked toward Shelter Island. "I don't even know if she's still there. She could have gone to stay with him in the city. Hell, they could have gone back to Rome for all I know."

"Let's cruise by," Sperry suggested, as if I hadn't already thought of that, hadn't already steered the boat in that general direction. It would take longer, but who cared. We had all the time in the world. There were two weeks left in August and suddenly I had no obligations.

"Can you see the house from the water?"

"Not really," I lied. My voice was slowing down. I never slurred, or at least I never knew if I slurred, but everything got much slower.

"Do you love her?" Sperry asked suddenly. Sperry never talked about love. Always sex and bodies and asses and tits. Never love. I'd never considered Sperry to be the emotional or sentimental type. Maybe he was growing up after all.

"No." I shook my head hard to knock the idea around a little. I'd hardly thought of anything else for days. I had no idea what the word even meant, but I'd come to the conclusion that what I felt for Elisabetta couldn't be love. It was too wrong, too forbidden to be that, too tainted.

"It was more like lust," I considered. "Obsessive lust." Finally, it was the truth. How could you love someone you hardly knew?

We glided over the flat waters of the Peconic. If I hadn't been so drunk I would have been more nervous about floating past Greenport, so close to Eddie's docks, but I had one thing on my mind: the scarf either waving from the turret or not. And if it was? What would I do then?

I didn't want to point out the old Victorian to Sperry, not specifically. But it was obvious when I slowed the boat as we curved around West Neck Point. It was the only structure for miles. I'd never seen so many lights on in the house.

And there it was: the bare turret. I could tell even in the fading dusk. We floated there staring at the monstrous place, at the yellow glow from the windows.

"Looks like she's home," Sperry said. He propped both of his feet up on the edge of the boat, his bright red shoes pointing into the sky like jaunty little lighthouses.

"Yeah," I managed.

I squinted at the house until the door and the windows with their wide old shutters became blurry. I thought I could make out a couple of figures in one of the front windows. Maybe a flash of long dark hair. I turned on the motor and moved about twenty yards closer to the shore. The fuzzy shapes took on the form of bodies, and I could make out Elisabetta's distinct silhouette, the curve of her hips and breasts. She was pacing the living room. Perhaps she was just waiting for me. Maybe the scarf had blown away. Maybe she'd turned on all the lights as an invitation. *I'm here. Come to me.*

I allowed us to inch ever closer to the shore. Sperry kept his mouth shut.

Suddenly Elisabetta filled the entire window. She stared out at the sea. Was she looking for me? Waiting? I knew that my boat was probably a mere dark speck from such a bright house, that we were nearly invisible. I squeezed my eyes shut and thought hard about her, willing her to see me through the inky blackness. But she only stared and stared. I opened my eyes.

A figure came up behind Elisabetta and grasped her by the

arm, pulling at her, almost violently, jerking her away from the window. Who was it? An intruder? Another lover? I couldn't imagine Hartwell, that tiny old man, grasping his wife with such force.

"Did you see that?" I asked Sperry in a whisper, even though the sound of the waves lapping the shore would drown out my voice even if we were closer to the house.

"Who was that guy?"

"I don't know."

"Do you think she's in trouble?"

I wonder if I would have done what I did next if Sperry hadn't been with me. If we hadn't worked each other up in a frenzy of macho heroism.

"You need to make sure she's all right," Sperry said. Yeah, yeah. The thought had already crossed my mind.

A terrible idea. We hadn't spoken since that night she told me she wanted to kill her husband. Elisabetta could be volatile when she'd been drinking. Who knew what kind of trouble she could get herself into.

You just wanted to play the hero.

Maybe you're right. I think I said it out loud.

"I'm going in there," I announced.

"You're going in there," Sperry echoed boisterously with confidence.

We pulled the boat up on the spit farther down West Neck. I gave Sperry very specific instructions on what to do. If I didn't return in thirty minutes I wanted him to take the boat back to Sag Harbor, tie her up, and go home. I'd make my own way back. There was a ferry from Shelter after all, or at least there would be in the morning. I was drunk enough not to worry about Sperry driving my boat. He was drunk enough he could do anything.

Was there a small part of me that hoped Elisabetta was in danger so I could be the one to save her? I didn't give a thought to what I must look like, my blue oxford stained with sweat and eel guts, my hair disheveled and filthy, my beard unkempt. I didn't bother with shoes, just trudged onto the sand as I heard Sperry crack open one of the last beers and settle in to wait for me.

Fireflies blinked through the trees. The house was even brighter from the shore. I tried to peer through the windows from a distance, but the two figures were gone. By the time I reached the front door I could hear music playing. There was no going back. I tried the front door and wasn't even surprised to find it unlocked. Had she ever locked that door? I stumbled into the foyer and almost tripped over a pile of sandy shoes, flip-flops, heels, worn leather boat shoes. I kept going, into the living room, drawn to the music. What was it? The Rolling Stones maybe. The foyer led to the hallway and the double-height French doors that opened into the living room. I found myself standing in that doorway and staring, mouth open.

Elisabetta's hair whipped through the air as she twirled across the floor and into the arms of a small but formidable man with steel-gray hair. Sam Hartwell grasped his wife by the elbow and spun her away from him while a crowd, most of them my parents' age and older, smiled and cheered. A few others danced. I could tell they were all drunk, like they'd been at this for most of the day. The night, with all of its promises, had just begun.

I watched Elisabetta grab Sam around the waist. He leaned into her to whisper something in her ear, and she threw her head back with laughter.

This woman didn't need saving. I stood there dumbly staring at them.

As she spun out of Sam's embrace she turned to the grand doors and finally spotted me, the look on her face a mixture of confusion and horror—maybe also a dash of sympathy.

"My lady," I croaked. "I've come for you." I sounded like a drama club understudy, an impostor. The music stopped; everyone turned to stare in my direction. I wished I could fall through the floor.

Sam squinted at me and pulled a pair of wire-rimmed glasses from his shirt pocket.

"I know you." He inspected me further. "Are you Maxwell Cane's boy? I've seen pictures of you in your father's office. Bette, did you invite the Canes? I thought they were in Paris for the summer."

Boy. I was just a boy. It rattled around, taunting me. *Just a boy. Just a boy.* I closed the space between us then, uncertain about what I was going to do until I did it. *I'll show him I'm not a boy.* I grasped Elisabetta's cheeks in both of my hands and pulled her face to mine, kissing her hard on the lips, ignoring the gasps of the partygoers. Her mouth was firm beneath mine, but she made no move to kiss me back. We stayed like that for only a second before she pushed me away.

Her hand flew into the air and she slapped me hard across the face. I felt a sharp pain in my lip, blood soon dripped down my chin.

"How dare you?" she said sharply. "I—I think you've mistaken me for someone else." Hartwell was in my field of vision now, standing by his wife's side. I expected him to strike me too and decided in that moment that I would let him, that I deserved it, that I wouldn't fight back. There was no anger in Hartwell's eyes, only a twinkle of bemusement. Perhaps this wasn't the first time some lustful stranger approached his wife, grasped her, and kissed her on the mouth.

"You *are* Maxwell Cane's boy," he decided after inspecting me further. "He's told me a lot about you. You're working for him in the fall, yes?"

If Elisabetta was confused she didn't show it. Her face maintained her perfect calm.

Hartwell motioned around to the rest of the party. "Nothing to see here, folks. Maxwell Cane's boy must have developed a crush on my beautiful wife." He glanced at her. "How sweet." He grasped her by her waist then, his fingers kneading into her hip.

Hartwell swiveled his head and kissed her neck. "I didn't expect such excitement this evening." He reached behind him, into the back of his trousers, and pulled out a brown leather notebook, long and thin, the right size to be carried around in a back pocket. His fingers found a pen that had been tucked behind his right ear and began to scribble on the pages.

"This has been grand." He smiled, seemingly to himself. "Perhaps I should put this scene into my new novel. Perhaps your father still wants to buy it."

Someone in the crowd stifled a laugh, and Elisabetta's expression changed for the first time. She blinked and lowered her gaze. Was it pity that she cast my way? I saw myself then as she must have seen me: nothing more than a boy, a pleasant distraction from her real life.

Get out. Get out. Get out. I stumbled as I turned toward the door, tripping stupidly over my own two feet. I grasped the wall and felt my way to the living room door. I knew they were watching me and I didn't care. Before I made it outside someone turned the music back on. The sounds of a party resumed, laughter, chatter, no doubt about me.

Instead of walking on the beach, I blundered through the

woods. Stubbed my toe on a low stump so hard I knew the nail would eventually pop off, but I didn't make a sound. How long had I been gone? I squinted down at my watch, hoisting it into the air to try to make out the shine of the gold dials in the moonlight. I knew without having to look that Sperry would be gone, a speck floating back to the next shore. Hopefully he made it. I had been so goddamned stupid to let him take the boat without me.

I walked all the way out to the edge of the point. The tide crept closer and closer to the tree line, pushing me into the woods. A group of kids were having a bonfire on Wade's Beach across the water. The South Fork felt so close from here, like I could swim there. I could see the orange cherries on the ends of their cigarettes, smell the burning driftwood, almost taste the cheap beer. But I knew better. Maybe I'd make it. Or maybe a current would crush me against the rocks or sweep me farther out to sea. Maybe I was too drunk and too tired and too defeated to do much of anything. Maybe I'd drown, and maybe I didn't give a damn if I did.

I let myself sit down on the edge of the trees, knowing the water wouldn't come much closer. Elisabetta had cracked me good in the face. Blood dripped from the wound. I tried to wipe some away with the edge of my hand and then used the tails of my shirt to apply pressure. I'd feel the pain in the morning. Of all the stupid things I'd done this summer, the mistakes I'd made, the careless decisions, this had to be the worst. What happened tonight could cost me my job, my future, my father's respect.

There was a part of me—a new part, I think—that didn't care at all.

CHAPTER SIXTEEN

My hands were covered in dried blood. Memories of the previous night flashed in my mind in hazy and disjointed bits like a damaged newsreel. My entire body ached, and my lips felt like someone had peeled back the skin. Water lapped at my feet as the sun beat down on my face. A seabird nibbled at a piece of dry kelp and let out an irritated squawk when I sat up and rubbed at my eyes. Judging from the position of the sun, I'd been asleep a long time, maybe ten hours, maybe more.

I half expected my boat to be within arm's reach, but then I remembered Sperry took her home. Oh God. I let Sperry drive the boat back to Sag Harbor bombed out of his brain. He could have floated halfway to Block Island by now. He could be dead.

The other memories came in waves. Fishing, drinking, crashing the party, getting cracked across the face. The way she looked at me. The way he looked at me.

The two of them dancing.

She was so happy dancing with him. It shattered something in me. It shattered the fragile idea I'd had of their marriage. Everything I'd thought about her, and her marriage, and her world . . . everything I believed had been wrong. If Elisabetta was truly happy with Sam, if the woman she'd been with me had been temporary, a costume she'd merely been trying on, then what did that make me?

Shame knotted my insides. How had I let it get to this? I wasn't this person. I'd played it safe my entire life, followed the rules, went to the right schools, kept my head down. My future was all laid out for me. A good job, a nice apartment, safe, secure, easy.

I'd become someone new with her. The kind of person who took risks, who didn't play it safe. I liked that person. I liked him a lot. I liked him despite the fact that he'd managed to ruin my entire life overnight. I still couldn't grasp entirely what that meant, what the consequences might be, but I knew it was true.

I needed to get home. I stared longingly at the water and made a decision. The tide was now low enough that I could swim across West Neck Harbor and be close enough to walk to the ferry dock to take me back to North Haven, to the North Fork. I wouldn't need to walk back down the point and past Elisabetta's house, risking the chance of her, or worse, Sam, seeing me.

Salt water burned my lip as I dove in. I like to think I abandoned him, this other me, Joe, as I shoved away from that goddamn island. But that wasn't entirely true. I could feel him and all the unfinished business like a weight I had to fight against in order to make it to the distant shore.

Mouths dropped in horror as folks spied me wandering the edge of the road, next to their well-manicured North Haven lawns, the ones surrounded by actual white picket fences. One guy was riding one of those tractor lawn mowers, clearly a novelty for him considering the size of his lawn and the fact that he probably paid an army of immigrants to take care of the rest of it. He wore nothing but swim trunks, showing off his wrinkled old man six-pack. When he saw me he actually flicked the back of his hand at me as if to shoo me across the street to soil someone else's side of the road. I considered hitchhiking into town, but if anyone stopped to pick me up it would probably be the police. I tried to relax. It was a free country.

I finally stumbled into a gas station on the edge of the town. A cheerful bell dinged my arrival through the service station door. The smell of burnt coffee assaulted my nostrils, and I wished I had even a crumbled dollar in my pocket. After the swim and night on the beach, the midmorning sun burning my face and back of my neck to a right crisp, I couldn't finish the five-mile walk to my parents' house.

The kid at the cash register was picking his nose when I walked in, really mining for something in there. I almost felt guilty for interrupting him.

"Do you think I could bum a quarter from you for a call?"

I had no money. I was lucky the Shelter Island ferry agent had taken pity on me and waved me past.

He withdrew his finger from his nostril and reached into his back pocket for some change. He flicked the grimy coin across the counter with his index finger.

I dialed my home number, hoping Sperry would pick up.

"Cane residence. How may I help you?" Was he speaking with a British accent? It actually sounded pretty believable.

"Do you always answer the phone with a British accent?"

"When I don't answer in Japanese."

I hoped to holy hell that my parents hadn't called when I wasn't home. "Can you come get me?"

"Shelter?"

"I'm at the gas station near the end of North Haven."

"How'd you get over here?"

"I swam. And then I took the ferry."

"Brutal! Did you save her, man?"

"Can I tell you about it when you pick me up? I had to borrow a quarter from the kid inside the gas station and it's gonna run out soon."

"Yeah. I'll be there. Give me ten."

I stared balefully at a sweaty Coke machine and thought about asking for the key to the bathroom so I could lap some water out of the faucet, but I didn't feel like going back inside. Instead, I rounded the corner, over by where they pump the air into tires, and sat down on the curb. Sperry made it there in less than ten minutes and began the interrogation as soon as I got into the car. I told him about Elisabetta dancing with Sam, my weak entreaty to her, the slap, the humiliation. I had to tell someone. Telling someone made it real.

"Who was at that party?" he asked. "Was my dad there?"

"Why would your dad be there?"

"That man loves a party. Especially now that he's single. He's always making a round of the old-folk parties from South to Shelter. He's making these last couple of weekends of the summer really count. He needs a new wife."

"I don't know," I told him honestly. "I can't remember. Parts of it are crystal clear, and other parts are hazy. I didn't get a good look at anyone."

"What a disaster." He said it with a chuckle. Maybe he liked the fact that, for one summer of our lives, I became a bigger screwup than him.

"Your mom called, by the way."

"Shit." I tried to calculate the time difference in Paris. If I had walked into Elisabetta's house close to nine last night it would have been three in the morning in Paris. Too late to ring my mother, even if Elisabetta had any idea how to reach her. Of course she could have called this morning, when it would have been afternoon there, but what were the odds?

"What did she want?"

"She wanted to remind you that you have a doctor's appointment in the city with Dr. Lindblatt. Do you still see our pediatrician?"

"She's a family doctor. She sees our entire family."

"I'm pretty sure she was our pediatrician. Does she still let you take a toy from the treasure chest if you're a good boy during your appointment? I miss Dr. Lindblatt. She had some great boobs. I used to try to get real close to them when she'd lean over with the stethoscope. I almost licked one once."

"Enough, dude. Seriously, stop it. You can't talk like that. She's someone's mom, daughter. She's a *person*. You gotta stop talking about women like this."

"Come on, bro." But he had the courtesy to look chagrined.

"Sperry. Just stop."

We sat there quietly for a second before I changed the subject. "That's all my mother said? She just wanted to make sure I went to the doctor?"

"That's it. Oh, and she told me to make sure you got your suit and shirt dry-cleaned for your first day of work. She said you can take it to the cleaner's by their house. She was real worried you would try to take it somewhere close to your new apartment. She says no one knows how to dry-clean anything properly below Fourteenth Street. She's worried you're going to get scabies."

"She didn't say scabies."

"She said a rash, which is the same thing. Does this mean you're going into the city tomorrow? Are you done? Is summer over?"

I'd planned to go into the city for the doctor's appointment, just an annual checkup I had to do for my new insurance, and then come back out for the last week before Labor Day. But things had changed. Every day out here would be a reminder of how badly I'd messed things up. There was no way I could stay out at the beach. Every day there I risked running into Elisabetta. The list of consequences for what I'd done were endless. Now that she knew who I was she had the power to ruin me, to ruin my reputation and my father's reputation forever if she wanted to. How would she behave if she saw me? Ignore me? Or what if my outburst at her house had been the last straw in her own fragile marriage and I found her alone, miserable?

I'd managed to fool myself into thinking I could run back to the city. Maybe there my lies would never catch up with me.

"I gotta go. It's time for me to get back." I paused and thought about Sperry out here all alone. "Be good. Okay? Will you re-member to have the cleaners come in before you leave? And re-place whatever good liquor you drank?"

He ignored my domestic instructions. "Really, dude? That's it. What about that girl on the North Fork?"

"Kit."

"Yeah, Kit. And her dad, Eddie. Aren't you even going to try to find out what happened to him?"

I desperately wanted to know what happened to him, to her. "They cashed the checks. He must have gotten the surgery. She never wants to talk to me again." I said it very matter-of-factly. I'd accepted it. I'd accepted all of it. I had to accept it.

"Come on, Sperry. Neither of these women ever want to talk to me again. I blew it with both of them. It's over. I'm going back to the city in a couple of hours. Stay at my house through Labor Day. My parents won't even bother checking on the place when they get back. Dad needs to be back at work, and my mom is going to be too busy organizing the public-library benefit. Just make sure it's clean and there isn't a speck of cat hair."

"Mrs. Frankweiler is an incredibly hygienic cat."

"I know she is, Sper. Just do it. Please."

"Yeah, yeah," he said. And in a rare moment of tenderness, he put his free hand on my sunburned shoulder. "Don't worry, dude. I'm on it." I knew he would be. That was the thing about Sperry— you could take him for his word. I used to think this about myself.

I was the only idiot escaping paradise on a Sunday, under no illusions that I wasn't just running away from all of my problems. I needed the city, the faceless crowds. I could disappear in them. There's this Dorothy Parker quote I love: "London is satisfied, Paris is resigned, but New York is always hopeful. Always it believes that something good is about to come off, and it must hurry to meet it." The idea of returning to New York made me hopeful that I could find a way to solve everything I had messed up.

The train to Manhattan was always empty early on a sunny afternoon. I leaned my head against the cool glass of the train window and made a silent prayer. If only my parents didn't find out about what happened with Elisabetta, about what I'd done the night before. If only I could avoid humiliating them and destroying my father's business, I'd do exactly what I was supposed to do. I'd live the life I was supposed to live. I repeated it silently to myself over and over as we passed beyond the emerald-green lawns, quiet forests, strip malls, car dealerships, on our way to the concrete jungle. I whispered it only once out loud as the train came to a grinding halt in Penn Station. *I will not fuck up the rest of my life.*

CHAPTER SEVENTEEN

I allowed the mundane details of organizing Henry Cane's grown-up life to distract me from the mess I'd made. I'd left Joe behind in the Hamptons. It worked only because I was descended from a long line of folks who bury their feelings in their to-do lists. I went to see the beautiful Dr. Lindblatt. She didn't offer me a lollipop or a decoder ring when I left, and I wondered if it was because of the beard. Maybe it was time to find another doctor, one closer to my new apartment downtown, one who didn't try to tickle me in my belly. I worked my way through my list with agonizing efficiency: dentist, dry cleaner's, renewing my gym membership, donating some books to the library, checking in with the movers. I started packing to keep me busy until boxes were stacked two high against the walls. Growing up my mother didn't like a lot of stuff in our house, and my room was no exception. So unlike most of my friends I didn't have *Baywatch* and Wham! posters tacked to my walls. They were painted a modest navy blue with white trim. I was allowed a few sailing models and track trophies on the shelves. Books were really the only decoration in the room, shelves and shelves of them. I hadn't yet packed any of them away because I couldn't decide which ones to bring to my new place.

I'd always thought that the books you owned defined who you were, or maybe who you wanted to be. The first thing I did when I walked into anyone's house was peruse their bookshelves, see what they kept and wanted others to see. I always wondered how many of those books were read or purchased for show or put down after a chapter or two.

I'd read everything on my shelves. I had a rule that I wasn't allowed to put a book on a shelf if I didn't finish it. Of course this led me to finish a lot of books I didn't truly enjoy. I stood and ran my hands over their spines now. It was all there, the Hardy Boys to Kafka. Maybe I wouldn't take any of them downtown with me. My new apartment had floor-to-ceiling bookshelves built into one wall in the living room. There was plenty of room for them, but building a new book collection seemed like a small way to start anew.

I worked with such efficiency that part of me was able to forget about the summer entirely. *What summer? What lies?*

Of course, late at night, staring at the faded glow-in-the-dark stars on the ceiling of my childhood bedroom, I knew I was fooling myself. I imagined Elisabetta calling my mother to tell her everything, or worse, Sam calling my father.

I thought about Kit silently seething, hating me for the rest of her life. I worried the money I gave her wouldn't be enough to save Eddie, that I'd failed even in the one good thing I'd done in the past two months.

It took hours before I finally dozed off into a fitful sleep.

The phone woke me up the next morning. Who calls someone at 7:00 a.m. on a Tuesday? Probably my mother. But I didn't make it out of bed in time, and the machine started beeping like crazy, too full to take another message.

The answering machine at my parents' house blinked red

with thirty-five messages, but clearly it seemed like an unwieldy task and I wasn't up for it. My mother's one bad habit is calling her own answering machine to leave a reminder for herself. She'll stop at pay phones in the middle of London to call home and remind herself to make a hair appointment for the following week. Over the years my father has tried to break the habit by buying her an array of beautifully bound Moleskine notebooks for her to-do lists.

"I have a system, Maxwell." She always snaps back using his full name instead of Mooks, her nickname for him. "And I've been running our household perfectly well for a quarter century. If you'd like to try out your lists, then be my guest. I'll hand the reins over to you. You can do it all." And then the answering machine would fill up again.

I rooted around in drawers of the sideboard until I finally found one of those notebooks my dad was always buying my mother so I could write down all the messages for her.

As I suspected, most of them were reminders *from* my mother. Call caterers for Young Lions event. Send birthday present to Ruby on September 15. Order red velvet cake for Mooks's birthday. Then there was the cleaning service calling to confirm that they would start back up cleaning the apartment in September, a couple of friends looking to schedule tennis matches.

But then: Sarah Knowles. Oh God, Sarah Knowles. "Deirdre," she began without any charm or niceties. "I don't know when you're coming home, but I have something I have to talk to you about. It concerns Henry."

It concerns Henry.

There it was. My reckoning. I played it over and over again. Part of me wanted to call Sarah Knowles myself to try to head off whatever she was going to tell my mother. I could use the excuse that I was hoping to set a date with her daughter.

I continued to beat myself up as the answering machine spit out the remainder of my mother's to-do list and the complicated tango of running our household.

Then, a low-pitched woman's voice.

"This message is for Henry. I think I have the right phone number. This is Katherine Delgado. I was calling with a message from my father . . . from my family. You can reach me at 631-555-4532. I won't be available at the office phone number."

Katherine. Her name was Katherine. It was a lovely name, but Kit suited her better. She wasn't a lovely girl—I had known and dated plenty of perfectly lovely girls—and Kit was something else entirely. Why did she use her full name in the message? How did she know the number? She must have looked us up in the phone book. I played the message back again to take down her number. I went into the kitchen to get myself a glass of water from the sink and finished half of it before picking the phone up again. It rang four times and went straight to her answering machine. "Hey, it's Kit. You know what to do." Now that sounded more like her. Her no-nonsense tone brought a smile to my face. I imagined myself back in her bed, my arm stuck beneath her, her body sweaty and stinking of whiskey and sadness. It had gone numb, my arm, but I stayed like that until I finally got up the courage to leave. Hearing her voice without the rough edge of disdain filled me with a startled relief.

It felt strange to leave a message on her machine. *Hello, this is Henry Cane calling for Katherine Delgado.* I thought about calling the hospital, but that felt presumptuous, and I had a feeling I should follow her instructions to a tee if I wanted to make any headway with Katherine Delgado. I tried the number again just after 5:00 p.m. I was about to hang up when the answering machine came on.

"Hey, it's—"

Then a breathless voice interrupted. "Hello. Hi. I'm here."

"Kit?"

"Who is—Joe? Henry?"

"Hey."

"Hey."

The *heys* lingered. Neither of us wanted to be the first one to speak. I'd been the one calling, but then I was returning her call, so I felt like it should probably be her instigating the conversation. I cleared my throat in the hopes it would encourage her, and in return she sighed, so I forced myself to talk.

"Katherine, huh?" I tried to allow some lightness in my voice. "I like Kit for you better."

A long pause. "You know, I never thought Joe suited you."

I smiled then for the first time in more than a week. She knew me better than I ever thought she did.

"Probably not. I should have thought of a better pseudonym."

"Or told me your real name." There was the signature Kit sarcasm. It was something.

"Or that," I said needlessly. I didn't want to make small talk. I'd never been very good at it, and I could tell it wasn't one of Kit's strengths either. "So why'd you call?"

"I think we should talk."

"Okay."

"In person."

My first instinct was to say, *Yes, of course. Anything.* But I was afraid too, and that reminded me what a coward I'd been. I was terrified that seeing her in person would strip down every amoral and reprehensible thing I'd done that summer. I was terrified I wouldn't be able to handle that.

"I'm back in the city now."

"I know. I called you there."

Be a man, Henry. Be a goddamn man. "But, I can come back out."

"Saturday."

"Okay."

She gave me an address, which I scrawled quickly in the notebook. I wrote down the house number on Kenneys Road, careful not to smudge the number. I promised to meet her at noon, tried to sound cool when I said it, even though the thought of seeing her filled me with warm and shy feelings.

"So. Great. I'll see you then." She hung up before I could respond, and I sat there dumbly holding the phone until it made a rude noise alerting me that I had better press the button and hang it up at once.

I should have insisted I would come out the next day or the day after. Why the hell did I agree to Saturday? It's not like I had anything to do for the next four days. I was packed. My teeth were clean. I'd dropped the suit at the dry cleaner's.

I spent the rest of the week walking and riding the subway. As a kid, I loved the subway so much that on Sundays my dad would let me pick a line and we'd ride the MTA from the first stop to the last while he'd read the entire *New York Times* and I'd stare at the subway maps. Now I rode all the way uptown and then walked the length of the island, all the way down to the Battery and back to the town house, and then the next day I did it again, same walk, except I went down Broadway instead of Madison and walked past the office on the corner of Fifty-First, where I'd start work in two weeks. In fourteen days I'd start going to that office five days a week. I'd wear a suit and a tie and take meetings and pretend I knew what the hell I was talking about. It almost didn't seem possible. I stared up at the building and thought about just going in and getting started. Why wait? But then I kept walking another fifty blocks.

I was starving by the time I got downtown and got in line at the dinged-up falafel cart in between the twin towers.

"Henry? What are you doing in the city?"

I turned to find Sperry's dad standing with a pretty young woman in a red suit.

"Hi, Mr. Cross," I said. "I was just going for a walk."

"I thought you'd be at the beach with Brett, enjoying your last days of freedom." He chuckled. His friend or colleague looked at me suspiciously, and I realized I still hadn't shaved my ridiculous beard. It's funny how adults always found ways to equate work with prison or some other form of getting locked away. They loved to tell me my days of so-called freedom were over. "Is Brett still at your house?"

"I came back early. Brett's staying through the holiday." We were nearly at the front of the line, but I suddenly wasn't hungry anymore. Seeing Sperry's dad gave me an idea.

"Here, you can order before me, Mr. Cross. I just remembered I need to make a phone call."

There was a pay phone on the mezzanine of the south tower. I dialed my beach house.

"Sperry, hey. So, I need another favor . . . from your dad."

I knew I'd made a mistake when I saw Larry standing next to Kit at the address on Kenneys Road. For the first time I realized just how much I had underestimated the magnitude of all my lies, everyone they reached and touched. A sneer slashed across Larry's broad features. Kit's older brother could knock me down with a single punch, a punishment for a snot-nosed yuppie punk who dared to infiltrate their world.

They both took in my car, the new-enough Mercedes convertible I'd been gifted by my grandparents when I graduated high school. I considered pulling away until Kit raised her hand in a small wave. Then I steeled myself to get what I deserved.

The man's sneer loosened into something else, not a smile exactly, but something a notch less menacing. When I got close enough for him to reach out and grab the collar of my shirt or sucker punch me right in my soft stomach, he instead reached out his hand.

"Thank you for saving my dad's life." I took it in disbelief, unsure what he knew and didn't know.

He continued. "Kit told me you come from across the bay. I never thought real high of them folks, but you proved me wrong. You're welcome here any time, Henry Cane." With that he walked away, back to his rusted truck, and left me alone with Kit, perhaps the more dangerous of the two.

"I wanted to thank you," she said simply.

"I thought you hated me."

"I did. I do. Or I did. I don't know. Look, you did a really big thing for us, and you deserve to be thanked. I'm not an asshole."

"I never said you were."

"So," she said, voice cracking a bit. "Thank you."

I softened my tone. "How is he?"

"He's good," she managed. "He had surgery last week, and that was hard for him. He's not the kind of guy who asks for help . . . you know."

I couldn't help myself. "I feel like that runs in the family."

There was a slight smile in her voice. "Maybe it does."

"Is that the only reason you brought me here? To this place?" I looked around the ruined old property, knowing it was the place Kit had told me about at Martha's. She'd been so honest with me that night, so nakedly honest about her dreams. Maybe she needed to show them to me in real life.

She remained coolly impassive. "It's as good a place to meet as any."

"Show it to me. Please." I let my voice crack on the last word.

With that she walked, and I dutifully followed.

"It was built in 1860," she began, her way of changing the subject. I swear she grew an inch from the pride she felt in showing me around. "See those cottages over there? Those could be little guesthouses." She motioned to a couple of worn-down shacks amid a bramble of thornbushes. I could see it when I squinted, but only because the excitement in her voice helped draw a picture in my head. I loved the delight in her eyes when she imagined the possibilities.

"They could be."

The main house looked like it could fall down if it was struck by a particularly heavy gust of wind. My interest in the old place seemed to put her at ease. It was wonderful, and Kit knew everything about it. She told me how it was once owned by a commodities trader who bet big on pigs at the turn of the century and made a ton of dough. But the place went to hell when the guy passed away without any kids. It made me think about what would have happened to Gatsby's place after he died on the raft in his pool. On the deck, ivy twisted around the intricate railings before climbing the porch to capture the second floor. It looked as though the earth was intent on reclaiming this building as its own.

We walked around the mucky pond, where a family of Canadian geese had taken up seasonal residence. I picked up a rock and tried to skim it across the surface.

"Don't mess with those geese," Kit warned. As if on cue the largest of the pack hissed and lunged toward me. I stumbled backward and fell ass-first into the mud.

"I warned you." Kit laughed for the first time in too long.

We kept trudging through knee-high weeds in silence.

"I don't bring many people out here," she admitted as we finished walking around the perimeter of the property. "Bringing someone here makes it feel real, like it might actually be possible some day. Does that make sense? And you—Knowing who you are. You're the kind of person who might understand what it would take to do something like this."

"I get it," I said, thinking about the mundane things I'd done in the past week to make my own future seem more obvious and clear. "What's your plan, Kit? What happens next?"

She squinted off into the distance as she came up with her response. "Dad finally agreed to sell the business. The boats, all of it. He listened to me." She was proud of that, I could tell. "He's gonna live with my brother. My brother's wife, Leslie, studied to be a nurse, but she quit school when she got pregnant. She still knows how to take care of him, though, keep him eating right and all that, physical therapy. It will be good for him to take a break, you know. It will be good . . ." She trailed off.

"But what about you?" I pressed her. Weren't Kit and I cut from the same cloth? We'd grown up desperate to please our families, our fathers. We hadn't developed the muscle that allowed us to please ourselves until very late in life. "What about school?"

She cast a shy smile at the ground. "I got a job. A good job. I'm excited about it actually. And Cornell said I could defer for a year, maybe even two years while I work to save up some money. Have you heard of the Baker House?"

I cocked my head to the side like I was trying to recall the place. Of course I knew it well. It was this luxurious bed-and-breakfast in the Hamptons, the kind of place people rented out for weddings. My parents spent their anniversaries there. My seventh-grade classmate Jackie Goldberg had her real fancy bat mitzvah there the summer we were all turning thirteen. I remembered it because Jackie got to arrive on the lush green grounds in a Bell helicopter and that was the summer I was obsessed with helicopters, so I was real jealous. Jackie's dad was a music exec, and he'd hired a cartoonist to re-create the A-ha "Take On Me" music video with drawings of Jackie and all her friends. Then the actual band showed up right after dessert and brought a stunned and understandably awkward Jackie onstage to sing with them. It all concluded with thirty minutes of fireworks and Jackie riding away from the property on a white horse with a horn attached to its forehead to make it look like a unicorn.

When Kit had first told me about her dream of opening her own bed-and-breakfast on the North Fork, the Baker House was the first place I thought about, minus the unicorn and one-hit wonder and braced-face kids running around.

She kept going; her face was flush with excitement, her hands fluttering as she described it. "They've got this program where they help workers go to school too. That's how they found me. They were looking for someone who was accepted to Cornell. I guess they talk to the school or something. I don't know how it all works. But that doesn't matter. So you know . . . that might help. Maybe I'll save enough to ship off next year."

I bit down on the inside of my cheek to keep myself from smiling and maintained a look of curious surprise. I knew I could never tell her that Sperry's dad had financed the Baker House's latest renovation and was now the hotel's largest stakeholder. It had been a small favor to ask after I'd put his son up all summer. It felt better to be a hero when no one else had to know about it. I wouldn't consider it a lie exactly, just an omission.

I'd never seen Kit look so happy, maybe an inkling of it that day with the dolphins, but this was different. That was pure joy in a singular moment. This was the release of anxiety, relief that life might actually have something exciting to offer when she'd long written off the chance to be happy.

"That sounds great." I smiled. "Maybe I'll even come out and see you sometime while you're working." I said it carefully, agnostically.

"Maybe you will." She nodded slowly, watching me. "Maybe that would be nice." She wrapped her arms around her slight shoulders and shivered against the sea breeze.

"Maybe we could even grab a drink sometime," I said, going out on a limb.

"We'll see," she said. "We'll see. It might be nice for me to get to know the real Henry Cane."

Yeah, I thought. *You and me both.*

CHAPTER EIGHTEEN

"Make me look like me again," I said to the man wielding the straight razor against my Adam's apple.

It required a proper barber to shave the monstrosity that had taken up residence on my face. George, the old Norwegian man who had been cutting my hair at the beach since I was five years old, visibly winced when I walked into his shop and sat in his red leather chair.

He cocked an eyebrow and let out a small chuckle, running his hand over his own bald head, as if he thought he might still have hair there. George reached over to touch the coarse wilderness dripping off my chin.

"That's a tall order." He wasn't just talking about the facial hair.

As long as I'd been coming to see him, George seemed to know things. When I was small he could tell when I'd gotten in a fight with my mother and he'd let me spin around in the barber's chair for ten minutes until I felt properly compensated for having to visit the barbershop. During my increasingly awkward puberty, George asked me my opinion about what I wanted my hair to look like. Did I want it a little longer in the back? A lot of the other boys were keeping their hair a little longer on the top. Did I want to try that? He was the first person to give me some small amount of agency over my appearance, my life.

George scrutinized the forest on my face, contemplating his plan of attack.

It took the octogenarian more than an hour, but he managed to clip and then shave and clip some more until I could finally see my face. It was nearly another hour before he trimmed my hair back to the old standard. Part of me had missed it, this simple haircut with an obvious part, seeing my face, my mouth. I looked just like every other guy I was about to go to work with. I tipped George double what I usually gave him and stepped out onto Main Street. Did I feel like a new man? I caught a glimpse of myself in the window of the bookstore. Not really. Maybe I was finally ready to accept that the old me was an okay guy.

I was never going to be one of those guys who took off and traveled around the world with all my possessions in a single knapsack. I'd probably never climb a mountain, or kill a man with my bare hands. I'd probably never even finish a novel. This summer I'd captained a fishing boat. I'd had an affair with a woman almost twice my age. I'd been spanked and humiliated, and I'd liked it. And then everything else. All of it. I'd helped a friend through a difficult time. I might have saved a man's life. Those things may not have been everyone's idea of adventure. For some people maybe that was just a Tuesday. But for me it was everything.

As I turned the corner to find my car I glimpsed the deeply tanned back of a beautiful woman, spine straight, perfect posture, thick brown hair pulled into a knot on the top of her head. She moved slowly, wheeling a small black suitcase, well assured of her place in the world. The sight of her still made my breath catch in my throat. I had two choices. I didn't have to stop her. I could let my memory of her and our time together stay as it was. I'd written her a letter of apology, but I didn't know how to get it to her without Sam possibly intercepting it. It remained in the drawer of my nightstand in New York.

I quickened my step and gently tapped her bare shoulder. I could see her body shudder at an unexpected touch, and she turned around slowly, ready to swipe a hand away or tell someone to screw off.

Her features contorted into an expression of irritation when she pivoted on her heel, and I could tell it took her a moment to place me without the beard, the long hair. Once she did her lips relaxed and her eyes blinked and danced just a little. She placed a warm hand on my arm and gave it a small squeeze.

"Oh. Henry," she said coolly and without an ounce of surprise. "It's nice to see you. I've been hoping I would run into you. I have glorious news for you."

"You do?" I hadn't expected her to be so friendly, but then she'd never once done anything that I'd expected her to do.

"I'm pregnant," she announced, kissing me on both cheeks and then pulling away, eyes wide and fixed on my face to watch my reaction.

I fell backward onto a bench in front of the hardware store. My insides twisted with panic. I clutched the bench so hard I thought I'd get a splinter. "R-really? How? I mean . . ."

She laughed, her mouth wide, her lips stretched thin over her white teeth. Blood pounded so hard against my temples that I hardly heard what she said next.

"No. Not really. Please. I'm practically in menopause." She bent over to pinch my cheek as she said this, clearly delighted to point out our age difference. "But your face is priceless, and I had to make a terrible joke. It was terrible, but also funny. Yes? You think it is funny? Imagine our poor child. So confused. Is she my grandmother?"

My breath eased, and I allowed a small chuckle that became an actual laugh because it *was* funny. She *was* funny. Her sense of humor was one of the things I'd missed the most about her. It was often dark and audacious and self-deprecating. She was unlike anyone I'd ever met before and anyone I would ever meet again, full of surprises. And yet so constant, so sure of who she was.

She sat down next to me and crossed her long legs, folded her fingers into her lap, and placed her hands almost primly on top of her thigh. When I'd been with her in her house I'd loved watching her hands, seeing her long, slender fingers move deftly over the ivory keys of the piano, picking parsley from the herb garden in the backyard, mixing paints, tying her scarf into intricate knots around my wrists, skimming the pages of an age-worn book.

"I will miss shocking you. You are so easy to shock. Maybe too easy, but it has been very, very fun." She reached into her purse and pulled out a small blue tin of lip salve. I watched her as she spread the clear paste over her pink lips. I could still remember exactly how those lips tasted.

"I am leaving though," she said. "I had hoped I would run into you before I had to go, and now here I am heading to the train station and here you are. Like you were waiting for me all along."

"For the city?"

"For Rome."

Rome. Of course. She hated New York. I said the first thing that popped into my mind. "Are you leaving Sam?"

Her eyes squinted in confusion as she tried to make sense of the question. "I'll never leave him."

"You told me you wanted to kill him." I lowered my voice to a near whisper when I said it, then I felt like a fool. It was all part of the game.

"I do sometimes," she said, and rolled her eyes. "But that's marriage. I love him. And sometimes I hate him. But the good thing is that we don't both hate each other on the same day. That's how we've managed to last so long."

Her honesty clawed at something inside me, how she put it all out there. I thought about my parents' marriage and everything I thought I knew about it and everything I didn't know about it. I thought about how one day I figured I would meet a woman and fall in love, really fall in love, and maybe marry that woman. I hoped that what Elisabetta was saying wasn't true. Not for everyone. But then, didn't everyone start a relationship thinking they would be different, thinking they would defy the odds?

"Does he know about me? About us?"

A flicker of amusement crossed her face when I said the word *us*, as if we ever deserved the pronoun.

"Oh, he thinks you are a sweet boy from across the bay from a good family who developed a crush on me." She smiled, satisfied with herself. It was the truth, after all.

Just a sweet boy. Somehow it didn't bother me. I was still attempting to be a man, trying my very best. The strange thing was that growing up I'd never once felt like a child. As the only offspring of two wildly independent and often self-interested people, I'd always been treated as an adult, and I'd strived to behave like one in the hopes that it would endear me to my parents. The definitions were still hazy to me. Boy, child, adult, man.

"Across the bay? You knew where I lived this entire time?"

"Of course."

"And you knew who I was."

She nodded like this was incredibly obvious.

"Since when?"

"Since the entire time. Mostly. You want to know when exactly? Let me see. Oh, that benefit. I saw you before you saw me, sitting at the table with all your school friends. I asked someone if they knew your name. The infamous son of Maxwell Cane. Scion to Empirical Press!"

I couldn't help but laugh. "I haven't done anything to make me *infamous*."

"That might have been true then, but it certainly isn't true now, is it, Henry? You are much more interesting than when I first found you."

"But you invited me back to your house again anyway, after that, even knowing who I was?"

"I liked you." She smiled. "I still like you. If you must know . . . I was curious about you."

"Even though I lied? You knew that I lied about who I was."

"Ah . . ." She sighed. "But perhaps that made me even more curious. Besides, everyone lies to everyone. It's how we survive. All of us. Anyone who says otherwise is a liar."

She spoke in these grand declarations, as though she had long ago figured out exactly how the universe worked and pitied anyone who disagreed with her.

There was something I needed to say to her. I'd been practicing the words.

"I'm sorry."

"Don't be."

"I was reckless, coming to your house that night, like that."

"We were both reckless." She stared hard at me. "I hope this doesn't stop you from one day being reckless again."

I knew I had nothing left to lose.

"I read your husband's manuscript. I found it . . . in that room on the third floor while you were sleeping, and I read it, or most of it anyway. I shouldn't have gone up there. I did. And I'm sorry."

Her brows rose. Had this surprised her? Was I a mystery to her after all?

"Did you enjoy it?"

I could talk about it all day. "It's the best thing I've ever read." I paused and looked her right in the eye. "His book . . . it's about you."

She nodded slowly. "It is."

"The way he described you on the page. It was glorious. It was you. It wasn't just a character. He made you come alive."

She clearly liked this. Who wouldn't? This was my only chance. It certainly wasn't the safe option, the good choice, but I was done with that. "Elisabetta . . . Who could possibly edit a book about you better than me?"

Her eyes lit up, but her mouth remained unmoved. She waited a beat before answering, very slowly, as if considering this fact to herself for the very first time.

"That's a good point."

I didn't want to appear too eager, but she'd opened the door. "Good enough?"

"That's the boldest thing you've ever said to me, Henry Cane." She laughed. "I like it. I like you like this. I have taught you well."

"So you'll talk to him. To Sam."

She laughed again. As long as I live I'll never forget the sound of her laughter. Joyous, sinister. Villainous and heroic.

She turned to face me full on, taking time to watch me. It felt like she could see into my brain, and I knew then that I was not actually one step ahead of her. Maybe she had already considered it. "Henry, Henry, Henry. Why the hell not. I have made crazier propositions to my husband." I had no doubt.

Part of me wanted to grab her by the shoulders and kiss her, hug her, take her back to her house even and make love to her for the rest of the day. But I didn't even move. Didn't even lift a hand. What existed between us in her house on the island felt like a distant memory, or something that happened to someone else, a character in a book that I loved so fiercely I could never bear to reread it.

There was one lingering question, of course.

"What about my mother?"

She furrowed her brow. "What about her? She is a lovely woman. I very much enjoyed spending time with her. You look like her. In the eyes mostly."

There was this small part of me that was ashamed that I was a grown man so concerned about what my mother thought of me. The other part was desperate that she'd never learn about what happened between Elisabetta and me, that she be allowed to think about me as an innocent boy as long as that was something that made her happy.

"Does she know?"

"Oh, Henry. You are still such a child in so many ways." Her words felt like someone pressing on a bruise that had always been there. "She will never know. The people at our house that night . . . they were old friends of Sam's and mine. They are not—how should I say this?—your parents' people. Perhaps that is why the party was so much fun. None of those beachy types. Mostly Europeans. They do not care one bit about all your silly gossip. They do not know you. In fact some of them thought you were a funny little actor I had hired to get a rise out of Sam! Can you imagine?" She put her hand on my shoulder. "I let people believe what they want to believe. You should too."

"So Sarah Knowles . . ."

"Oh God, no. I told that old crone to skitter off. No more profile of me. I am not very interesting anyway."

She was wildly interesting, and we both knew it. But someone like Sarah Knowles could never capture precisely how.

I felt a tremendous lightness suddenly when I hugged her. She hugged me back like we were old friends. I suppose by then we were, in our own way. Maybe one day we'd be back in some other house, laughing about this all over a bottle of her favorite red.

"You know, Henry Cane," she said as she stood and smoothed her skirt, preparing to leave. "I know many things about you. I can tell that you are a man who appreciates smart women, strong women—a man who loves them, needs to be around them." She reached out to stroke my newly smooth cheek, letting her finger trace my top lip, stopping in the middle and placing it over my entire mouth like she was telling me to be quiet for a moment more. "Never lose that. It is the very best part of you and will serve . you well in life." She punctuated the sentence with a low chuckle.

"Thanks, Bette. I won't."

She walked toward the station. I knew she knew I'd watch her until she disappeared, and that maybe after that I would close my eyes and see her still.

Only once she was completely out of sight, once I could no longer smell her perfume in the air or feel the warmth of her hand on my skin did I realize that she had finally called me a man.

ABOUT THE AUTHOR

Charles Brooks is an editor and publisher. He lives in New York City with his two daughters. This is his first novel.

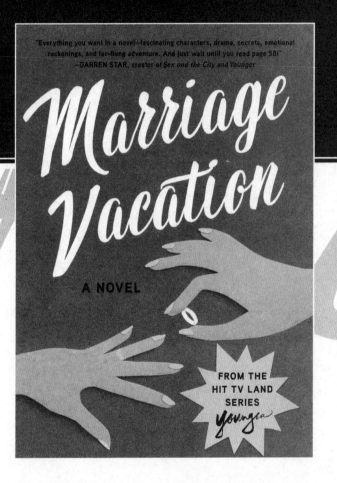